res
judicata

res judicata

Vicki Grant

ORCA BOOK PUBLISHERS

Library and Archives Canada Cataloguing in Publication

Grant, Vicki
Res judicata / written by Vicki Grant.

Sequel to: Quid pro quo.
ISBN 978-1-55143-940-2

I. Title.

PS8613.R367R48 2008   jC813'.6   C2008-903051-6

First published in the United States, 2008
Library of Congress Control Number: 2008928570

Summary: Cyril MacIntyre is on the case again, working for his eccentric mother and giving new meaning to the term "legal aid" in this sequel to *Quid Pro Quo*.

Orca Book Publishers gratefully acknowledges the support for its publishing programs provided by the following agencies: the Government of Canada through the Book Publishing Industry Development Program and the Canada Council for the Arts, and the Province of British Columbia through the BC Arts Council and the Book Publishing Tax Credit.

Design by Teresa Bubela
Cover image by Dreamstime.com/Bruce Collins

ORCA BOOK PUBLISHERS
PO Box 5626, STN. B
VICTORIA, BC CANADA
V8R 6S4

ORCA BOOK PUBLISHERS
PO Box 468
CUSTER, WA USA
98240-0468

www.orcabook.com
Printed and bound in Canada.
Printed on 100% PCW recycled paper.
11 10 09 08 • 4 3 2 1

This book is dedicated to you, Jeannie Richardson, because
1. You threatened me and
2. *Te valde amo ac semper amabo.*
Mudge

acknowledgments

I could never have written a book about the law without help from my friends in the legal business. I'd like to thank Joy Day for setting me straight about what deputy sheriffs do in Nova Scotia. I owe my old buddy Phil Campbell a couple of vacation days to make up for the time he spent on the dock at Stony Lake explaining the intricacies of criminal law to me. My husband, W. Augustus Richardson III, answered my endless questions (including "How do *you* know?") and hardly ever looked irritated. It is in thanks for this and his many other roles in keeping me on the straight and narrow that I have recently elevated him to the bench.

Needless to say, any mistakes that slipped through into these pages are entirely mine, not theirs.

V.G.

chapter 1

The guy had his hands around my neck and was slamming my head against the floor. I guess he couldn't decide whether he wanted to strangle me or bash my brains in.

Either that or he'd just got tired of killing people the usual way.

I tried my best to fight him off, but what a joke that was. Me, Cyril MacIntyre, AKA Mr. Puniverse, was going to take down a tank like him?

Right.

SpongeBob would have had a better chance against Mr. Clean. To tell you the truth, I was kind of impressed that I even made his eyeballs bulge. At least it showed I wasn't a total wipeout. At least I made him work that much.

Any other time, one swat upside the head would have flattened me. The only reason I was holding my own this time was because I was so mad.

Not at him. I mean, I kind of expected it of *him*. What was he supposed to do? I was asking for it.

The person I was really mad at was my mother. This was her fault. All her fault.

As usual.

If Andy—that's her name—wasn't so hard to get along with, she wouldn't have ended up on the street when she was fourteen.

If she wasn't so—let's say—careless, she wouldn't have had me when she was fifteen.

If she wasn't so competitive, she wouldn't have had to prove she could go to law school when she was twenty-five.

If she wasn't so cheap, she wouldn't have dragged me to all her night classes. (I mean, would it have killed her to spend ten bucks occasionally for a babysitter? She spends more than that every day on her French fry habit.)

If she wasn't such a worrywart, she wouldn't have made me stay up every night helping her study.

If she hadn't been all those things, if she'd just been a normal boring person like mothers are supposed to be, I wouldn't have known anything about the law.

And if I hadn't known anything about the law, I wouldn't have said anything.

And if I hadn't said anything, I wouldn't have had a big greasy pair of hands around my neck. My brain wouldn't have been ricocheting off the back of my eyeballs. I wouldn't have been seeing that weird white light and hearing one of those deep manly angel voices calling, "Come home, Cyril! Come home!" I'd have been down at the skateboard bowl, just hanging out, doing what your average fifteen-year-old likes to do: nothing.

Frankly, I'd had enough of Andy messing up my life. I wasn't going to let her get away with it again. Suddenly I could hardly wait to get my hands on her.

I guess that's what I needed. A goal. Something to look forward to. I got this burst of strength. It wasn't superhuman strength or anything handy like that, but it was enough. I bent the guy's thumbs back a millimeter or two. My windpipe popped open. I sucked in this little whistle of air, looked him right in the eye and said what I needed to say.

"*Res judicata.*"

chapter 2

Factum
A statement of the facts and law to be referred to, which is filed by each party in a legal application, appeal or motion.

Five months earlier

The first time I saw Dougie Fougere with Andy, I figured he was arresting her.

That's not as crazy as it sounds. I bet everybody was thinking the same thing. I mean, who wouldn't be? You see a cop run down the street and grab some skinny emo chick in army boots, you naturally expect him to cuff her.

If you're the kid of the emo chick, you then naturally expect her to elbow him in the teeth and add "resisting arrest" to whatever other charges she's facing.

What you *don't* expect is for the cop to put his arm around her neck, lean his big, water cooler head right into her face and then—I'm not kidding—nuzzle her ear.

My faith in reality could have been saved at this point if Andy had hauled off and smoked the guy, but she didn't.

She *nuzzled* him back.

By the time I recovered from the shock, I was ready to arrest the both of them. "Nuzzling" might not be covered in the criminal code, but it should be. After all, there are laws against public indecency, not to mention cruelty to children. (If watching two adults—one of whom is your mother—nuzzle in public isn't cruelty to children, I don't know what is. Frankly, I doubt the emotional scars will ever heal.)

Luckily, Andy came up for air long enough to see me standing there glaring at them. You'd swear her dad had just caught her necking on the front porch or something. She hurled herself away from the guy and then tried to do this blinky baby bunny thing with her face. Like that was going to make her look innocent. I just shook my head. How gullible does she think I am?

She got all fake and vice-principally on me. "Oh. Why. Hello. Cyril. I didn't expect to run into you here."

"You didn't?" I said. "You mean, that little performance wasn't for *my* benefit?"

She tried to say "What?" as in "Whatever do you mean?" but I just kind of coughed out this laugh. No way was she getting away with that, and she knew it. She adjusted the rip in her T-shirt and tried to smile.

I could practically see her brain racing around, opening up drawers, checking under cushions, rummaging through pockets, trying to find a new tactic to try on me.

She finally just turned to the guy and went, "Ah…Dougie, this is my son, Cyril."

The guy's eyes sort of popped, as if he was trying to hold down a major burp or something. "Son?" he said. "You didn't tell me you have a son."

Clearly, the old truth tactic wasn't working so well either.

She gritted her teeth into a smile. "Of course I did!" She turned and stood in front of the guy. I couldn't see her face, but I know her well enough to be pretty sure her eyes were doing that voodoo thing to his brain. It's the ultimate submission hold. She can pull people's fingernails out with that look. In the end, everyone talks.

The guy started nodding and went, "Oh, right, *that* son! Of course!" He reached out to shake my hand. "How you doin', Sport?"

Sport?

I mean, seriously. *Sport*?!

What am I—a beagle or something? I can't believe these big guys. You'd think it would be enough that they get to block our view with their beefy, well-defined physiques. Do they really have to treat us like we're cute too?

I just let his hand hang in the air. After a while he shrugged, put it on his hip (as if he'd been planning to do that all along) and said, "Well, I guess I better take off if I'm going to be ready for that...ah...you know...*thing* tonight."

Andy didn't even look at him. She just went, "Yeahokayseeyagoodbye."

They both sort of raised their hands as if they were going to recite the Boy Scout pledge or something. Then Andy turned and walked away. I could still smell the guy's cologne coming off her. What did he do, roll in the stuff?

Andy grabbed me by the arm, all perfect little PTA mother, and said, "So-o-o...how was school today?" Apparently I'm cute and easily distracted too.

I acted all forgive-and-forget. I smiled. "Really interesting," I said. "We discussed some of the unexplained mysteries that have baffled scholars throughout the ages."

"Coo-o-l. Like what?" She loves thinking she produced some brilliant little sit-in-the-front-of-the-class brainiac kid. You wouldn't know it from the "nuzzling" incident but, generally speaking, she takes this whole mothering stuff *way* too seriously.

It's like I'm her big term project or something, and she's going to get an "A" on me even if it kills one of us.

"Oh, you know," I went. "Mysteries like how the pyramids got built…or what happened to the dinosaurs…or how some radical left-wing wacko like Andy MacIntyre ended up dating a cop. You know, that kind of stuff."

She dropped the whole PTA thing so fast you could practically hear it smash on the sidewalk. She sucked her lip up into her nostrils and snarled at me. "He's not a cop!"

"Sure looks like it to me."

"He's a deputy sheriff!"

"Ooh. Big diff."

She bugged her eyes out and sighed so loud you'd swear she was launching a blow dart at me. I almost ducked. She went, "Cyril…Floyd…MacIntyre! Surely you've spent enough time in courtrooms to know the difference between a cop and a sheriff!"

Here it came. The lecture. Another one of her favorite diversionary tactics. I made myself comfortable and let her get it out of her system. It wasn't as if I could stop her.

"*If* you'd been paying attention, you'd remember that in Nova Scotia at least, sheriffs and their deputies are peace officers, not police officers. They work in the court system. They carry out judges' wishes, keep order in the court, escort prisoners to and from the holding cells—that kind of thing. Cops, on the other hand, investigate crimes, make arrests, fine traffic violators, patrol the streets, issue noise violations, etc., etc., etc."

She sort of laughed. "You're never going to see a sheriff on the street doing that kind of hands-on stuff."

It was almost too easy.

I said, "Looked pretty hands-on to me."

That got her. She scrunched her mouth up so tight it looked like the knot on a balloon. "Listen, mister," she said. "You can't talk to me that way. I'm still your mother. So you better just *watch...your...mouth*!"

Can you believe her? Me? Watch *my* mouth? She can't see the irony in that? Who's the one who swears like a rap star around here? Who's the one with the three contempt-of-court citations? And, oh yeah—whose mouth was just nuzzling some sheriff's ear?

Exactly.

"I mean it!" she said. "So you better just smarten up. And by the way"—she walked ahead so she wouldn't have to look me in the face—"I have a little something I need you to do. That factum on the Iqbal file has to be written up by tomorrow morning."

I've got to stop here and explain something.

In case you haven't noticed, Andy's got guts. Not just nerve, gall, gumption, the run-of-the-mill stuff. She's got guts coming out her ears. Not literally—at least most of the time—but you know what I mean.

Sometimes that's good.

For example, that old Mr. Zed guy and his twenty-two cats would be living on the street if Andy hadn't had the guts to take his big fancy landlord to court.

Spotless Drycleaners would still be dumping their not-so-spotless toxins into the harbor if Andy hadn't had the guts to sue them.

And, to tell you the truth, I'd probably be in a foster home today if Andy hadn't had the guts to raise a kid all by herself, go to law school, keep us fed and mostly out of trouble. Emphasis on "mostly."

But there's the downside to her having guts too.

Like this, for instance. I catch her red-handed with some guy in the middle of the street and she actually has the guts to tell me *I* have to stay in all night and do *her* work.

Please. Like, seriously, I wasn't the one around here who should be grounded.

I suddenly felt like the Incredible Hulk right before he bursts out of his shirt. I totally exploded. I went, "No way, Andy! That's *your* job!"

"It was. Now it's yours." She made it sound like she was giving me a present.

"How come?!"

"Because I can't do it. I'm busy."

"And I'm not? Trust me, I've got better things to do than sit home, putting some legal document together for you."

"Oh. Really? Like what?" She turned and looked at me all suspicious, as if she had just caught me up to no good.

I wasn't going to let her turn the tables on me. It might work for her in court, but it wasn't going to work here.

"No," I said. "Not a chance. You first. What do *you* have to do tonight that's so important you can't write that factum yourself?"

She fiddled with her rings. She held her hand out and checked her nails. (You'd swear the chipped black polish was just the look she was going for.) She cleared her throat. "Well, there's, ah…"

"No. Stop. Let me guess," I said. "There's that little, ah, *thing* tonight."

She started rifling through her purse for her cigarettes. "No!" she went. "It's not that. Why would you think that?

It's just that there's…Oops, sorry. Just wait a sec while I light this…Disgusting habit…I really should…"

I couldn't take it anymore. I went, "Would you quit stalling! We both know you're going out with that guy tonight!"

She looked up from her cigarette. She squinted at me. She licked her fingers and put out the match with this loud *pschhht*. By the look on her face, my guess is she was imagining the match was my head.

I said, "Why don't you get Atula to write the factum for you? She's a lawyer. She's your partner. Ask her."

She flicked the ash off her cigarette. She looked down the street as if she was suddenly wondering where her bus was or something. She went, "I'd rather not. I don't like to, you know, disturb her."

Yeah, "disturb" her by letting on that you're getting behind in your work again! No, Atula wouldn't have liked that. She wouldn't have liked that at all. It's just the two of them, running their law firm out of some cheesy little office over a fish-and-chip shop on Gottingen Street. They've got too many clients in too many bad situations not to stay on top of things. Atula figured that out ages ago. Why hadn't Andy?

Why did I have to be the one worrying about junk like that? She's the mother. She's the lawyer. I'm just a kid. I'm supposed to be worrying about my skin (which I do), about girls (which I do), about school (which I don't, at least not much). This was adult stuff. It wasn't fair.

And it wasn't fair that I couldn't even let her see that I was worried about it. The last thing I needed right then was Andy worrying that I was worrying. That would just make me worry more. I only had one option: block it out, do what I had to do.

I spun around and started to pace in front of her like I was some big-time courtroom lawyer addressing the jury on *Law & Order*. "So let me see if I've got this right. You expect *me* to spend the whole night writing up some legal argument on one of your files—that's right, *your* files—just so you can go out with your cop boyfriend?"

That made her wild. "I told you. He's NOT a cop and, for your information, he's NOT my boyfriend! We're just… ah, friends."

"Right," I said. I knew she was lying. She wouldn't get that mad if it weren't true. "I have a video project for my media arts class that I was going to get started on tonight, but that's okay. Don't you worry. Not a problem. I'll write your factum for you."

That weird orange glow went out of her eyes. The poisonous fumes stopped oozing out her nose. She got all misty.

"You will? Oh, C-C! I knew I could count on you!" She took her cigarette out of her mouth and threw her arms around my neck. She started kissing me all over my face. I hate it when she does that. If the embarrassment or second-hand smoke doesn't kill you, the nose stud will.

I peeled her off me. "All right. All right. All right. Save your public displays of affection for the Boys in Blue," I said. "I'm not finished. I'll write the factum for you *IF* you promise to buy me a new long board." I figured I may as well get something out of it too.

She stumbled back and gawked at me with her mouth wide open. She looked like she was choking on a bone or something. She even made that gacking sound.

"Are you blackmailing me?!" she said. "Your own mother?!"

I stopped and thought about it for a second. "Yeah," I went. "I guess you could say that."

She gagged on that bone again. "This is unbelievable! I'm…I'm…stunned! We're family! We help each other!"

"Right," I said. "My point exactly. I'm helping *you* by writing a factum so that you can go to that 'thing' tonight with Biff the Sheriff. You're helping *me* by using some of the money you're charging for the factum to purchase a skateboard. Some people might call that blackmail. I call it fair pay for fair work."

Andy was doing that twitchy thing she does when she's cornered. She took a big haul on her cigarette and wound up for a major rant, but we both knew it wouldn't get her anywhere. She didn't have a leg to stand on.

"Okay," she said and blasted this jet stream of smoke out the side of her mouth. "Be that way. There'll come a time in your life when you'll look back on this and be as shocked as I am now. You'll be appalled to remember how, instead of relishing the opportunity to work on a case that could save a deserving family from being deported to their war-torn homeland, you exploited the situation for your own personal gain. You thought nothing of the sacrifices your mother, *who loves you more than anyone or anything on earth*, has made to give you the life you have today. No. None of that mattered to you. You saw a chance to get rich quick, and you leapt at it. Fine. I have faith that some day you'll be mature enough to shudder at your behavior. I'll wait patiently until then for your apology."

Right. Like Andy has ever waited patiently for anything. You should see her lunge at the microwave when the popcorn's ready. She's like a piranha at a Mom 'n' Tot swim class.

"In the meantime, get that factum done—to my standards!—and I'll, like, buy you the stupid skateboard."

Most kids would have been happy with that, but not me. I knew who I was dealing with. Like any good lawyer, Andy was no doubt already looking for a loophole.

I wasn't going to let that happen.

I opened my backpack and took out the video camera I'd borrowed from the school media lab. I made her repeat her promise, this time with her hands out front so I could be sure her fingers weren't crossed. I even got a girl walking by to witness it on video.

No way was Andy worming out of this one.

I practically skipped home.

I never realized extortion could be so much fun.

chapter 3

Disturbing the Peace

The unsettling of proper order by creating loud noise, fighting or conducting other unsocial behavior.

About three weeks later, I was down at the skateboard bowl one day after school. Kendall Rankin, my best friend, was having trouble with a back wheel and stopped to fix it. I stopped to fix mine too. Not that it would do much good. I could have given the board one of my kidneys, and I still couldn't have saved it. I'd written that factum for Andy like I said I would, but I still didn't have a new board.

We sat there in the shade for a while, working away on our boards. Kendall's not much of a talker. His job is to sit there looking good and attract the girls. My job is to keep the conversation going. Usually I just stick to sick jokes and movie reviews. I don't know why, but for some reason that day I started telling him about Biff.

Ever since that "thing" he and Andy went to, Biff had been at our place all the time.

It was really bugging me.

He was really bugging me.

That day, for instance, Biff had showed up in his uniform and bulletproof vest at six in the morning *to take our garbage out*!

I went, "Like what's with that? It's *our* garbage. Not *his*! Doesn't he have his own? He has to go manhandling other people's? I mean, can you believe the guy? Let him sort his own recyclables!"

Kendall went, "Hm. Yeah. Gee," and went back to tightening his axle. He was trying, but I could tell he wasn't all that sympathetic to my situation.

I obviously hadn't explained myself very well.

So I told him about the love seat Biff just "decided" to "give" us because he didn't "need" it anymore. I told him about the way Biff always hums when he does the dishes and how Andy hums along, even though she has always *hated* people who hum. I told him about how Biff irons his jeans with creases so sharp he could use them to slice the sukiyaki at Tokyo Steak House and, more importantly, how *Andy has never even mentioned it.*

Kendall went, "Really. Huh. No kidding?"

I was starting to feel kind of stupid. There was this long silence. I considered mentioning the fact that Biff insisted on cooking us dinner every night—as if we weren't capable of feeding ourselves, as if there was something wrong with take-out burgers and fries!—but I didn't. My guess was that Kendall wouldn't understand that either. I decided to just let the whole conversation drop. I clicked my tongue and sighed like it was no big deal; then I went, "Whatever. I don't know why the guy irritates me so much, but he does."

Kendall put down his board. "Yeah. I know what it's like. I felt the same way when Mom started going out with Eddie. It took me, like, months to get over being jealous."

My head spun around so fast it took my eyeballs a couple of seconds to catch up.

I was like, "Jealous? What?! You're saying I'm...*jealous*?"

"Yeah. Not, like, boyfriend-girlfriend jealous but, you know, jealous. There's nothing weird about it. It's perfectly natural."

Perfectly natural. I hate it when people say that. They never mean it. In fact, they mean exactly the opposite. Just think of all the stuff they say in health class is "perfectly natural." It's never "watching TV is perfectly natural" or "liking peanut butter is perfectly natural." It's always the weird stuff, the stuff that nobody ever wants to admit to, that they call perfectly natural.

I didn't say anything.

Kendall went, "I mean, it's just been you and Andy all your life, and then suddenly some guy comes along and, like, horns in on the two of you, monopolizes her—you know, makes himself at home. Who wouldn't be jealous?"

The answer was obvious.

"Me! That's who. I'm not jealous! Don't make me barf. Jealous of Andy and Biff? Please. You make it sound like I want to spend all my time with my 'mommy' or something. The truth is, I spend most of my time trying to get *away* from her. I couldn't care less if Biff 'monopolizes' her. He can monopolize her and have Park Place and Boardwalk too! I'll even throw in my 'Get out of jail free' card. He'll need it if he's going to hang around with her."

I had to stop and wipe the sweat off my face with my T-shirt.

"That's not why I don't like him. It's just...I don't know... It's just...I mean, come on! The guy *irons* his jeans! Of course he's going to bug me! I'm only human!"

Kendall was already putting his helmet on. He shrugged. "Yeah. Sorry. You're probably right. I never had to put up with that kind of stuff with Eddie. His jaw clicks when he chews, but otherwise he's okay. I mean, he makes Mom happy. I figure after everything she went through when Dad left, she deserves to be happy now."

He got up. "Okay. You ready?"

He rolled back down into the bowl. He was my best friend. Now he was bugging me too.

I picked up the hunk of junk I call a skateboard and went home.

chapter 4

Child Labor Laws
Legislation that protects children by restricting the type and hours of work they perform.

I pushed open the door. I smelled chicken.

I knew it.

Biff was at it again.

I kicked off my shoes and walked down the hall. Andy was lounging on our "new" love seat, reading *The Catcher in the Rye* for like the four hundred and thirty-third time. She tossed it on the broken TV we use as a coffee table and said, "Hey, you're home late. Where were you? Down at the bowl?"

She smiled.

I didn't.

Since when did she smile when I went to the bowl after school? What happened to the "don't you have homework" lecture? Too busy for that these days? Got something better to do? I just ignored her.

I gave this big sigh. "Don't tell me it's chicken again! Who does Biff think he is? Colonel Sanders or something?"

Andy scrunched up one eye and hissed at me. "I've told you before. Don't call him that. His name's not Biff!"

Biff poked his head out from the kitchen. He was wearing a *Kiss the Cook* apron over his also-ironed T-shirt.

He went, "Hey! Whoa! Andy! What're you doing? You crazy?"

Andy hesitated for a second. It was all I could do to keep from laughing. Biff didn't know it yet, but I figured he was toast. Nobody pokes their nose into our family business and gets away with it. Nobody tells Andy what to do. My guess was she was going to boot him out of there before the skin was crispy on the drumsticks.

I stood back and waited for her to blow, but she didn't. She just looked up at Biff and smiled again.

Smile. Smile. Smile. What did she think this was, the Miss Congeniality Pageant?

"What do you mean?" she said, all ha-ha-ha.

"Oh, come on! Think about it," he went. "Which would you rather be called? Dougie or *Biff*?" He said it out one side of his mouth with this big blast of air.

She laughed. "You got a point."

"Hey, I can't take any credit," he said. "It was Sport's idea. Smart kid you got there." He raised an eyebrow and wiggled his head around. "Biff Fougere. Yeah. I like that."

He waved his spatula at me. "Now c'mon, Sport! Wash your hands. Grub's on the table."

I was getting the distinct feeling that I'd lost this round.

I fumed all through supper. Not only did I have to put up with my best friend accusing me of being jealous; I also had to sit there while Andy and Biff interrogated me about my buddies and my classes and my favorite movies and stuff like that. I had to eat another one of Biff's "wholesome" meals, and I couldn't even ask for seconds in case he started thinking I actually liked it.

I woofed the food back and then just had to wait around until they were finished. (There was no way I was leaving those two alone together. The nuzzle-o-meter was forecasting a major disturbance.) I started reading the newspaper.

Andy pretended that having the *Herald* spread out all over the table while she was trying to eat didn't bother her. "Anything interesting happening in the world today, C-C?"

My normal response would have been to just sort of grunt in her general direction, but then something caught my eye.

"Why, yes," I said. "In fact, there is."

I spun the paper around and pointed to a big ad for Boarders' World. "Whaddya know? You're in luck! Long boards are on sale. This week only. You can finally pay me for that factum I wrote!"

Andy did one of those laughie sighs and went, "Skateboards! I don't know why you want a new skateboard! The one you have is perfectly good. Now, Dougie—I mean Biff—could I have a little more of those delicious—"

"No, it's not!" I went. "And, anyway, that's totally beside the point. You *promised* me a new board!"

I'd interrupted her. I'd spoken in a disrespectful tone of voice. And I'd nailed her on that promise. She might not blow up at Biff, but she sure would at me. I prepared for blastoff.

She just flattened out her eyebrows and shook her head. "Do you have any idea how many toxic chemicals go into making those things? All that resin and fiberglass. It's disgusting! Honestly, skateboards must be every bit as bad for the environment as nuclear warships or suvs. Really." She looked at Biff. "Aren't I right?"

He went, "Well, that might be a *bit* of an exaggeration…"

I went, "See!"

She just sort of chuckled at how cute guys and their tiny brains can be. "Okay, well, maybe not quite as bad as SUVs, but when you consider that skateboarding is primarily a male sport—"

I went, "What are you talking about?! There are plenty of girls down at the bowl! Why do you think I go there? And what does that have to do with the environment anyway?"

Andy was trying to sound all calm and reasonable. "Nothing. I'm just saying, when you factor the toll on the environment in with the sexist nature of the sport, you start thinking differently about skateboarding. You understand what a huge negative impact it has on society, and you realize that you should avoid it at all costs. That's all I'm saying."

She smiled and dug back into her mashed potatoes.

I stuck my chin out and barked like some guard dog on a chain. "All you're saying is you don't want to pay up!"

"That's not what I'm saying at all." She dabbed the corner of her mouth with her sleeve as if she was the Queen of England or something. "I'm just noting that, after much reflection, I have begun to have some moral qualms about contributing to a sport that is so at odds with everything I believe in…"

Biff had been pretty quiet up to this point. He *splopped* another big cow patty of potatoes onto her plate and said, "I don't know, Andy. Seems to me there's lots of good stuff about skateboarding too. It's great exercise. It gets the kids outdoors. It…"

He didn't understand. Logic wasn't going to work. He was just giving her time to come up with another lame argument.

This called for the big guns.

I went, "Oh, we're talking moral qualms, are we? Well, I'm having some moral qualms myself! As you know, there are child labor laws in this country, a minimum wage and strict rules against practicing law without a license—all of which you broke when you made me write that factum! Frankly, I can't help thinking the law society might like to hear about some of your business practices…"

I grabbed the phone. "I believe their twenty-four-hour complaint line is 423-1…"

Biff went, "Whoa, whoa, whoa, there. Let's not do anything we might regret." He took the phone from me and put it back on the counter. I was all ready to tell him to butt out, but something about his face made me stop. It was like he was sending me coded messages through his eyebrows or something.

He turned back to Andy and said, "You know, Sugar, one of the things I love about you is that you're such a moral person."

Andy was looking at him, but I know she was mentally sticking her tongue out at me. She loves being right.

He sat down and put his arm around her. "I'm afraid this time, though, morality's on Sport's side. You *did* promise him a skateboard if he wrote that factum. I know because I saw the video—and the factum. To tell you the truth, I thought he did a pretty good job on both."

Biff must have realized he'd gone a step too far there. He said, "Smart kid. He obviously takes after his mother." The guy was smooth.

Andy's lips had turned into a perfectly straight line. She wasn't happy. I could tell Biff knew that too, but he just kept smiling and rubbing her shoulder with that big hand of his.

With the other one, he tapped the newspaper ad. "You know, $89.99 sounds like a pretty good deal to me. And look! It comes in blue, yellow and 'neon freak-out,' whatever that is. I think it's worth looking into."

Andy tossed her hair back and twitched her chin up a few times, but something in that old anger-management class must have gotten through to her. Either that, or Biff did. She took a big nose full of air and looked down at the paper as if she was actually going to consider buying the skateboard.

Biff leaned way back in his chair and gave me a big thumbs-up. I'd have smiled except Andy might have seen me. She'd have been screaming "Conspiracy!" then for sure.

He clunked his chair back down on the floor, slapped his knees and said, "Okay then! While you're looking at that, why don't I dish out some of my famous apple crisp? Sound good, Sport?"

I nodded.

"Great! What about you, Andy?"

She didn't move. She just sat there, hunched over the paper, like some crazy monk in an old horror movie or something.

"Andy…?" he said. "A little apple crisp? Andy? Yoohooo!"

He touched her arm.

She looked up from the paper. She had this wild gleam in her eye.

She said, "This is amazing! Un-be-lievable!"

I had a sudden, horrible glimpse into the future. How could I have been so stupid? This was just the type of thing she'd do.

I went, "Oh, no. Oh, no you don't! Don't even *think* about taking up skateboarding! No mothers allowed. Strictly forbidden. Off limits. Haven't you seen the signs?"

She waved her arm at me. "Skateboarding? Forget skate-boards! Look at this!"

She *shushed* the paper back toward me and pointed at an article right above the Boarders' World ad.

chapter 5

Manslaughter
The unlawful killing of a human being without malice or premeditation, different from murder, in that murder requires malicious intent.

"HERO" JANITOR CHARGED WITH MANSLAUGHTER

by Julia Rivers
Court Reporter

Last year at this time, Halifax Regional Police called university maintenance man Charles (Chuck) Dunkirk a hero. Now they're calling him something else: the accused.

Yesterday, the publicity-shy forty-eight-year-old was formally charged with manslaughter in the death of world-famous American inventor Ernest Sanderson.

It's an odd twist in a story that started out as a heart-warming tale of personal sacrifice.

Dr. Sanderson's invention of Gleamoccino, the widely popular coffee drink that "whitens your teeth while you drink it," made him one of the world's wealthiest men, but his true passion was for something considerably less glamorous: the Atlantic sea louse.

It was, in fact, this tiny crustacean that brought the Stanford-educated biologist to Halifax last year for a three-week research stint. During his short visit to the city, the 66-year-old Dr. Sanderson became better known to Haligonians—and their traffic cops—for his high-speed cruises down Spring Garden Road in his vintage Lamborghini convertible.

Late in the evening of February 4, just three days before his planned return to California, Dr. Sanderson was working alone in a lab at Chedabucto University. No one else was in the building at that time except Chuck Dunkirk, a janitor in his second week on the job.

Mr. Dunkirk had just sprinkled a powdered cleaning compound on the third-floor hallways when he heard a cry for help. He ran toward the noise and saw Dr. Sanderson trying to put out a small fire. In an attempt to smother the flames, Mr. Dunkirk threw the cleaning compound on the fire.

Unfortunately, the cleaning compound exploded and caused the fire to send off a thick black smoke. Mr. Dunkirk fought his way through the noxious gases and managed to drag Dr. Sanderson out of the lab. Mr. Dunkirk called 911, but by the time emergency personnel arrived seven minutes later, the visiting professor was dead of asphyxiation.

Mr. Dunkirk himself was treated for smoke inhalation and released from hospital the next day.

As word of the tragedy spread, Mr. Dunkirk was hailed as a hero. Despite worldwide media interest, the soft-spoken Cumberland County man steadfastly refused any recognition for his actions. In his only phone call with the press, he passed on his condolences to the Sanderson family and maintained that he was not a hero—"just a simple boy from backwoods Nova Scotia."

Now, at the urging of Sanderson's grieving widow, Chuck Dunkirk has been charged with manslaughter. The announcement of the charges sparked an angry protest yesterday outside the

Halifax Courthouse. About a dozen protesters marched with signs declaring "Chuck Dunkirk is not a murderer."

"I absolutely agree," said Crown Attorney Michael Lambert, who brought the charges against Mr. Dunkirk. "Chuck Dunkirk is not a murderer. A murderer kills his victim on purpose. No one is claiming Mr. Dunkirk meant to kill Dr. Sanderson. We recognize, in fact, that he was actually trying to save him. Unfortunately, although Mr. Dunkirk meant well, we contend that he should have known better than to throw an explosive substance on a fire. That's why we have no choice but to charge him with manslaughter."

Manslaughter is defined as the unlawful killing of another without "malice aforethought." In order to win their case, the Crown will have to prove that Dr. Sanderson died because Mr. Dunkirk did not act "with the care and caution of a reasonable person in similar circumstances."

Asked how difficult that will be to prove, Mr. Lambert said, "It's a pretty straightforward argument. The bag of cleaning compound was clearly marked with a printed warning as well as the international symbols for combustibility and poison. Mr. Dunkirk was a trained maintenance man. We feel confident that a jury will decide that his use of the compound on the fire was negligent and, as a result, will convict him of manslaughter."

The trial date has been postponed until Mr. Dunkirk can find a lawyer to represent him.

chapter 6

Indictment
A written accusation charging an individual with
an act that is punishable by law. A charge.

Andy was in legal heaven. A janitor charged with
manslaughter for risking his life to save some big-
shot celebrity inventor? I mean, it was her dream
case! It had everything she ever wanted. Rich against poor.
Educated against uneducated. Some guy who made millions
on a tooth-whitener against a genuine hero.

She was so outraged by the whole thing she could barely
wipe the smile off her face. "*Charging* a guy who tried to save
someone's life?! It's ridiculous! They're only doing that because
Sanderson had money! What is this—Verdicts-R-Us or something? Did Sanderson's widow just put it on her 'charge' card?
You'd swear nothing's changed around here since the Middle
Ages! Seriously. The rich still totally own the legal system!"

Biff went, "Now, Andy..." but that only cranked her
up more.

"No, really! I mean it! Can you imagine this happening
the other way around? What if it was the famous rich guy
who tried to save the janitor? You think they'd charge *him*
with manslaughter? Huh? No way! There's no *beeping* way
they'd even try!"

Biff kind of flinched at that. I'm not sure if he just didn't like her language—she'd been pretty good about swearing since he'd shown up—or if he didn't agree with her.

I don't know. Maybe living with Andy all these years had me brainwashed or something, but I couldn't help thinking she had a point. I doubted the police would have had the guts to handcuff some fancy professor guy who regularly showed up on *Entertainment Tonight*.

Before the ice cream had even melted on my apple crisp, Andy had tracked Chuck Dunkirk down and talked him into letting her be his lawyer.

And that was pretty much the last I saw of her for months. She'd rush home for a couple of minutes at suppertime, nag me (with her mouth full) about table manners, homework and dental flossing, then race back to the office to work on the case. She'd never been so happy in her life.

Biff had his own key and would sort of drop by whenever he wasn't in court. My guess was Andy was getting him to keep an eye on me, but he never made it seem that way. If you didn't know any better, you'd have thought he was there because he liked to be.

He actually didn't seem like such a bad guy, once I got past that whole GI Joe thing he had going on. He was pretty good at card games, but not so good that I couldn't beat him most of the time. His taste in TV was okay. He realized that seeing the latest episode of virtually any show on the air was way more important than watching coverage of Andy's trial. And even those wholesome meals of his were sort of growing on me. The closest my mother had ever come to making a chicken dinner was sprinkling some simulated flavor on my bowl of Mr. Noodles.

There was something else I kind of liked about the guy too, but it took me a long time to put my finger on it. It wasn't as if he was really funny or really smart or handing me twenty-dollar bills all the time. It wasn't anything obvious like that.

I couldn't figure out what it was.

Then one day, Biff was humming away, cleaning the compost bin that I was supposed to de-slime about a month earlier, and it just hit me.

I sort of liked him because, I don't know, he just seemed normal.

Andy was always slamming the door at you or throwing her arms around you or laughing her head off or refusing to let you see her cry. She was like this apartment we used to live in. The place was either boiling hot or so cold the water in the toilet froze. Never anything in between. It was like that until Andy took the landlord to the tenancy board and they made him put in a new thermostat.

That's what Biff was like. The Human Thermostat. He kept things nice and even. He didn't get all wound up and mad about anything. He'd just say, "Looks like your room could use a cleaning, Sport," and I'd look at it and think, Yeah, guess you're right. He'd say, "Try the asparagus with a squeeze of lemon. Bet you'll like it then," and I would and I did. He even had me convinced it made sense to do my homework *before* I watched TV, although how he did that, I don't know. I don't remember him actually ever mentioning it. Something about him just made you sort of want to do the right thing.

It was clearly a form of mind control, but that was okay with me. He had it working on Andy too.

She still bugged me about flossing and school and stuff, but I could almost hear her smiling underneath. She still worried about all the so-called injustices in the world, but she didn't ruin dinner over it anymore. She even looked kind of different. I mean, no one was ever going to mistake Andy for a soccer mom, but at least they weren't mistaking her for Marilyn Manson anymore either.

It was almost like being part of a real family. Ever since Biff showed up, I could sort of mentally walk around in my T-shirt, if you know what I mean. I didn't have to worry about being burnt to a crisp or frozen out. I was finally living in the temperate zone.

Then one night we were just hanging out at home, Biff and me, sitting on that love seat of his, sharing an extra-large Railroader's Pizza (the only store-bought food he could stand) and watching TV. I'd just bet him five bucks that the fish-eyed hairstylist from Orillia was going to be voted off the island, when a news bulletin came on.

I didn't know it then, but the weather was about to change.

chapter 7

Contempt of Court

Behavior in or out of court that violates a court order or otherwise disrupts or shows disregard for the court.

Breaking News with Jeff Leonard!

Jeff: Good evening. This just in: After three contentious weeks of courtroom wrangling, the Hero Janitor Trial… is over. The five-man, seven-woman jury deliberated for six long days over the fate of custodian Chuck Dunkirk. The question before them: Should this simple Good Samaritan be convicted of manslaughter in his ill-conceived attempt to save the life of Gleamoccino inventor, Dr. Ernest Sanderson? With the verdict and on-the-spot coverage, here's Eva Jackson—coming to us live from the courthouse steps! Eva.

Eva: Jeff.

Jeff: Tell us. Are Chuck Dunkirk's hands clean—or, in a cruel twist of irony, did the jury blame this whole dirty mess on the janitor?

Eva: Jeff, only moments ago, the jury gave Charles Bickerton Dunkirk their Good Housekeeping Seal of Approval and pronounced him "not guilty"!

Jeff: It must be a huge relief to Mr. Dunkirk to have the allegations against him "swept away." Can you describe the scene in the courtroom when the decision was announced?

Eva: It was a real "dustup," Jeff. Throughout this high-profile trial, Judge W. Augustus Richardson III went to great lengths to ensure the proceedings didn't turn into a media circus. He banned cameras from the courthouse, he issued several contempt citations to unruly spectators and he did his best to protect the privacy of Mr. Dunkirk—the timid, uneducated man at the center of the trial.

But none of Mr. Justice Richardson's entreaties could quell the outburst that rocked the court when the "not guilty" verdict came down. Chuck Dunkirk's lawyer, the always colorful Andy MacIntyre, threw herself on her client's back and issued triumphant victory cries, her fist pumping the air like that of a winning quarterback.

On the other side of the courtroom, Sanderson's glamorous young widow and former Miss Gingivitis USA, Shannondoah Boswick-Sanderson, broke down in loud gasping sobs, seemingly unconcerned about the devastation this outpouring of emotion would have on her carefully applied makeup.

Jeff: So unlike her. A moving testimony to the terrible grief she must be experiencing. Has she recovered?

Eva: Yes, she's had a few moments to touch up her mascara and she's here with me now. Shannondoah, thank you for taking time out of your busy day for the award-winning CJCH news team.

Shannondoah: You're welcome.

Eva: First off, the question that's on everyone's mind: Who are you wearing?

Shannondoah: My outfit?…Oh. Um. Versace suit. Gucci blouse. Manolo shoes.

Eva: And the bag?

Shannondoah: This? It's just an old Power Powder bag.

Eva: No, I mean your purse.

Shannondoah: Oh, sorry. It's Kate Spade.

Eva: Lovely outfit, and so appropriate. The charcoal gray suit says "widow" but in a very "now," very accessible way. And speaking of widows, as the fourth wife of the dead man, how did you feel about the verdict?

Shannondoah: Devastated. As far as I'm concerned, Chuck Dunkirk got away with murder.

Eva: You mean manslaughter.

Shannondoah: Murder, manslaughter, whatever. Either way, Ernie's dead—and it's Chuck Dunkirk's fault! The guys from the fire department said the fire in the lab was just teeny-tiny until that so-called hero went and tried to "rescue" Ernie. Like, what was he thinking? I mean, look. See what it says here in big giant letters?

Eva: Can you focus in on the bag for us, George? For those at home, it says "Power Powder. Danger. Do not place near flames or source of heat. Flammable. Combustible. Extremely toxic when heated. Inhalation could cause death."

Shannondoah: Exactly! Not hard to understand, is it? Even a bimbo like me got it right away. But what does Mr. Dunkirk go and do? Does he say to himself, "Gee, maybe I should find myself a fire extinguisher or a hose or a glass of water or something and put out this little itty-bitty fire"? No, he goes and throws poison stuff all over it! We're talking *kaboom*! So much for saving Ernie's life!

Eva: This is obviously upsetting for you.

Shannondoah: Yes, it is. *Very* upsetting. But do you know what upsets me even more than how Ernie died?

Eva: Those little lines you get all over your face when you cry?

Shannondoah: No...

Eva: Oh, sorry. What is it that upsets you more?

Shannondoah: Chuck Dunkirk did something that killed my husband, and now everyone's calling him a hero! Well, Ernie was a hero too. He did so much good in the world—for me, for others less fortunate, for...

Eva: There, there, Shannondoah. Don't cry. Can somebody take her for me? Thanks... Jeff, I think Shannondoah made a very good point. To anyone who ever suffered the agony of a dingy smile, Dr. Ernest Sanderson *was* a hero. So many of us, myself included, owe not just our personal happiness but our careers to Gleamoccino. Sanderson's death was a tragic loss for all of us in smile-dependent industries such as television news gathering.

Jeff: I think it's important to mention, Eva, that Dr. Sanderson's passing was no doubt a great loss to sea louse-dependent industries as well. We can't forget them.

Eva: No, we certainly can't, Jeff. Now, while Shannondoah is pulling herself together, I'll just walk over here and have a few words with Andy MacIntyre, lawyer for Chuck Dunkirk. Andy, my guess is that you have a very different take on the trial. How are you feeling about the verdict?

Andy: I think the best way to sum it up is what I said in the courtroom: *Whooo-hoo!*

Eva: Yikes. Sorry about the feedback there, folks. So, Andy, can you tell us how Chuck reacted to the verdict? He wasn't quite as, ah, "vocal" in the courtroom.

Andy: Yes, well, Chuck's a simple guy. He's happy, of course, but now he just wants to get back to his regular life. You know, scrubbing, dusting, looking out for his fellow man and/or woman. That kind of thing.

Eva: Your thoughts, now, on the trial. It took the jury almost a week to come to a verdict. Were you worried at all that the decision would go the other way?

Andy: Yeah, sure I was worried—worried about the world in general! Like, c'mon! You got this guy who A) volunteers to work an extra shift, B) risks his own life to save some stranger he's never laid eyes on before and then, C) turns down all the recognition offered to him because he doesn't think he deserves it—and it takes a jury six days to decide NOT to convict him?! I mean, what's the *beeping* world coming to? They should have thrown the prosecution's case out in two minutes and given Chuck a medal! What was the jury doing in there, playing Scattergories? Having a pajama party? Getting their highlights touched up? They sure couldn't have been thinking about the case all that time!

Eva: Your client didn't take the stand in his defense during the trial. He's avoided all contact with the media, refusing interviews, photo ops, a made-for-TV movie of his life. Any chance, now that his name's been cleared, that he'll consent to an interview with the award-winning CJCH news team? Maybe even a photo. We'd certainly love to get to know him better.

Andy: No way. Not Chuck's style. I'd be happy, however, to make myself available to CJCH about this or any other legal matter.

Eva: Yes, ah, well, thank you. And now, back to you, Jeff, at the CJCH Breaking News desk...

Andy: Stop! Over here, camera guy! George! Whatever your name is! Thanks. Sorry. Am I on-screen again? Okay. Can I say just one more thing?

Eva: Oh, ah, certainly, I guess.

Andy: Hi, Cyril! Hi, Honeybaby! Kisses! That's my son. Cyril MacIntyre.

chapter 8

Malicious Prosecution
Intentionally and maliciously pursuing a legal action against a person without probable cause.

C huck Dunkirk had little mashed-potato spitballs hanging all over that mountain-man beard of his. I knew it had to be hard keeping food in your mouth when you're missing most of your teeth and everything, but I got the feeling he wasn't even trying. I mean, the guy was like a snowblower.

I could barely look at him. I was going to be having nightmares about this for weeks.

Too bad. I *had* to look at him. I had to be on my best behavior. It was all part of my plan.

Or should I say *our* plan.

The dinner was actually Biff's idea. He convinced me that if we did something nice to celebrate her big victory, Andy would be in just the right mood to finally run out and buy that long board she owed me. He even promised to ask her about it himself.

I made him swear he'd do it as soon as everyone went home that night. You've got to act fast with Andy's good moods. Generally speaking, they have shorter life spans than your average sneeze.

I'd cooked and cleaned and peeled for three hours, all in preparation for finally meeting the famous Chuck Dunkirk. I couldn't let a little pre-chewed potato come between me and a new board. I had to make nice.

We were all squeezed around our puny kitchen table. Biff and I had dragged it into the living room so everyone would have a place to sit. Atula Varma, Andy's law partner, and Chuck got the place of honor on the love seat. The rest of us each got a kitchen chair and enough room for one elbow on the table. All I can say is it was a good thing Biff spent most of his time in the kitchen.

I looked up. I smiled like the perfect son I am. I still wasn't used to this Chuck guy. He just didn't look the way I expected him to look. The only time I'd ever seen him in the paper or on TV, he had his hands over his face. The reporters always talked about how timid he was. "Timid," "publicity shy," "humble." Those were the kind of words they used. It's stupid, I guess, but somehow I figured he was going to be smaller. I mean, timid is a little-person word. You know, more mouse than moose.

Chuck wasn't a little person. He was as tall as Biff but, as my geography teacher would say, "had a much larger land mass." To tell you the truth, he kind of looked like Santa's younger brother, the one with the criminal record. He had the whole bowl-full-of-jelly thing happening, and the beard too, but you could tell by Chuck's face that life hadn't been as cushy for him as it was up at the North Pole. He had no front teeth, a big doughy nose and bags under his eyes that—no kidding— looked exactly like those raw chicken breasts I'd spent the afternoon stuffing.

He sure talked a lot for a timid guy too. Someone asked him about his background, and next thing you know, he'd given us every detail about his childhood in backwoods Nova Scotia except for how often he changed his bearskin underwear. It was pretty boring but it didn't matter. I kept on smiling. He was a hero. Andy had won the biggest case of her career. I was going to get my board. What's not to smile about?

Atula didn't seem to hold it against Chuck that he got ninety-two percent of the love seat they were supposedly sharing. She asked him what his plans were now that the trial was over. Somehow that reminded me of my plan to hit Boarders' World first thing Saturday morning, and I drifted off before I could hear his answer. Just to seal the deal, I looked over at Andy in my most deserving-child kind of way.

I almost laughed. Andy had so many little blobs of potato in her hair, she looked like she was starring in her own Christmas TV special. The blizzard obviously didn't bother her at all though. She had an expression on her face that most people save for a marriage proposal or a winning door on *The Price Is Right*. Her eyes were all glittery, and she was so excited her head was vibrating like it was getting ready to blast off from her neck. She slapped the table and went, "Of course, Chuck! Brilliant! Why didn't *I* think of that? We'll make the police pay for what they put you through!"

Chuck did this aw-shucks thing and went, "Well, I don't know how brilliant it ith, Andy. I might be wrong, eh? I'm juth a thimple guy with no education or nothin', but I bet we could win a malithuth prothecution thuit."

He licked his middle finger and pushed his glasses back up his nose. He gave this big gummy smile. It was amazing. I could see all the way to that little punching-bag thing at the back of his throat. If I'd had a flashlight, I could have told you what he had for breakfast.

Atula started twiddling that scarf she always wears, and I knew there was something she didn't like about whatever the heck it was he just said.

"Chuck, might I offer an opinion? Suing the police for malicious prosecution is, of course, an interesting idea, but it would be a most difficult case to make. One would have to prove that the police had no basis whatsoever for charging you with manslaughter—that, in effect, they were just charging you to be unkind."

She stuck her lips out and shrugged. "I cannot see how you would manage to do that. It has already been ascertained in a court of law that there were adequate warnings on the cleaning solution, that you yourself threw it on the flames and that this alone was the cause of death of the unfortunate Dr. Sanderson. In my opinion, that's proof that the police had more than enough reason to charge you. Luckily, your very talented lawyer was able to convince the jury that in the heat of the moment you made a mistake—one that any reasonable person could have made—and you were found not guilty. I would be tempted to count my lucky stars and leave it at that, dear boy."

Andy laughed at that. "Yeah—but you know what? I'd be tempted to go for it!" It was pretty clear from the crazy-dog froth at the corner of her mouth that she wasn't going to be put off by a little thing like whether she could win or not. "I mean, hey, what have we got to lose?"

Atula scooped some Chuckie chunks out of her water glass with a spoon. "Well, for one thing, Andy, a considerable amount of time. Something like this could be dragged through the courts for years. Who will pay for that?"

Andy waggled her head around like "big deal." "I'll do it on contingency," she said.

Atula took a long breath in through her nose and made her lips sort of smile. She didn't like that idea either. Andy pretended not to notice. Something was up. It was making me nervous.

"O-kay," I went. "Two questions. 'Contingency.' A: What does it mean? And B: Is it even legal?"

Andy laughed. "Oh, Cyril! Of course it is. It just means that Chuck doesn't pay me anything while I'm working on the case. Instead, I'll get part of the money the court awards him when we win."

"*If* you win," Atula said. "You will receive nothing, of course, if you lose. Moreover, while you're working on the case, you will have no time to spend on your paying clients."

Andy opened her mouth to counterattack but was cut short by Biff walking in with a big pumpkin cheesecake.

"Sorry this took so long, folks," he said. "Had a little trouble getting it out of the pan."

Atula went all over-the-top about how delicious it looked. She wasn't lying, but my guess is she was only going on about the cake because she didn't want to get into an argument with Andy right then.

Fine by me. After all, the whole point of the dinner was to keep Andy in her best board-buying mood.

Luckily, a big hit of sugar usually takes her mind off more important things. Andy took a bite and moaned about how fabulous the cake was. Chuck made some lame pun about us finally getting our "just desserts." He had to repeat it a few times before we understood what he was talking about. I did some mm-mm-good thing too and smiled at Biff.

I was expecting a big grin back, but he didn't even notice. He was looking at Chuck.

It was only for half a second—not even that, a quarter of a second!—but I saw something happen.

I saw something go between Chuck and Biff. A look or maybe just a feeling, I don't know. It happened so fast I couldn't describe it. It was just there and then it wasn't, like a guppy in a fish bowl or a shadow when you're home alone. If they'd been smiling, I would have thought it was a private joke, but they weren't smiling.

Somehow I got the sense that whatever had just gone between them wasn't funny, and it wasn't something anyone was supposed to see either.

I looked at Biff. I pulled back my chin and kind of screwed up my face like "What was that all about?" but I was too late. By that time, Biff had gone all Biffy on me again. He winked at me. He mussed up my hair. He went, "Hey, Sport, give yourself some credit! You were the one who crushed all those graham crackers, not me. It's the crust that makes the cheese-cake. Aren't I right, folks? Not a bad effort for a rookie, eh?"

He nudged Atula with his elbow. He cut another piece of cake for Andy. He acted like nothing had even happened, and I probably would have thought so too, except for one thing.

For the whole rest of the meal, Biff didn't look at Chuck once.

Not once.

I mean, I sort of couldn't blame him. Chuck was pretty bad with the potatoes, but he was like some sick new Super Villain with that cheesecake. ("From out of his gaping jaws, the fearful Regurgitron spews orange radioactive sludge on his cowering victim. 'Take that, you thavage!' he roars.")

It was pretty disgusting, but somehow I couldn't believe that that's what was bothering Biff. He didn't seem like the type to get grossed out by a little thing like pumpkin boogers. The guy had a steel stomach. I mean, he cleaned that compost bin without even gagging. (I don't know how he did it. Honestly. The bin was like a cross between a port-a-potty and a scene from *Saw*.)

And there was something else too. Biff worked five shifts a week in the courthouse. He must have seen worse things there than Chuck's table manners. Like, seriously. Trust me. Not everyone who ends up in front of a judge is a movie star on a designer drug charge. Sure, you get rich people, but you also get poor people, tall people, short people, homeless people, crazy people, all kinds of people. I seriously doubt everybody Biff dealt with in court had a full set of teeth and knew how to use them.

Unless I was really wrong about Biff, there was something else going on here.

I was flicking back and forth between Biff and Chuck, mulling this all over, when Andy asked me if I still had that video camera from school. She wanted some footage of our little celebration. Chuck and Atula both put up a big fuss about getting their pictures taken, but Andy badgered them into it. I guess it's hard to say no to someone when you're eating dinner at their place.

I was looking through the viewfinder when I figured it out.

Chuck was still blabbing away. Andy was sitting there, smiling and wiping and gazing at him like he was the most fascinating man on the planet. She batted her eyelashes at him. It was probably just to shake off some of the graham cracker crumbs he was spraying all over her, but it looked kind of flirty anyway. That's when it hit me. I thought of what Kendall said at the bowl that day.

Of course! It was so obvious.

Chuck was "monopolizing" Andy. That's what was happening.

Biff was *jealous* of Chuck!

I had to bite my lip to keep from laughing. I mean, adults are *so* weird.

Chuck had no front teeth, questionable hygiene and a beard that in any other situation could have been mistaken for roadkill. The guy might have been a hero, but he was no hottie, that's for sure. Seemed to me, Andy was way too shallow to fall for someone like that. It didn't matter how many lives he'd tried to save.

I could hardly wait to bug Biff about this one. He would so squirm. It would be hilarious.

He was just putting his coat on to drive Chuck and Atula home. I went, "Ah, Biff. There's something I'd like to talk to you about when you get back." I tried to look all serious, but my mouth kept struggling free.

He went, "Can it wait, Sport? I want to talk to your mom about something later too." He lifted his eyebrows and smiled.

I couldn't believe it. I was so excited about torturing Biff that I'd almost forgotten about the long board. (Priorities, Cyril! Priorities!)

"Yeah, sure," I said. "No biggie. We can talk about it tomorrow. I'll just get these dishes cleaned up. Then I'll wipe down the counter, floss my teeth and go straight to bed."

I'd be embarrassed to be that sucky around my friends, but my friends weren't there, and I didn't care. I was this close to heaven. I pictured myself heading down to the bowl on my new board and the girls all sort of turning around to get a better look. One of them—probably Mary Mulderry-MacIsaac—would say something like, "Hey, Cyril! Niiiiice board. Where did you get it?" and that would be my, like, you know, entrée. We'd talk. I'd make a couple of jokes. She'd laugh and kind of flip back that black hair of hers. It would be excellent. My life could finally get started.

I had the table almost cleared before the door had even shut behind Biff.

I practically bounced out of bed the next day. Andy was already up, standing at the sink, waiting for the kettle to boil.

I didn't want to press my luck and ask her about the board, especially before she'd had her first hit of coffee. I figured it was safer to get the good news from Biff.

I poured some Cap'n Crunch into my glass of milk and took a swig of breakfast. I went, "So, ah, when's Biff coming by today?"

Andy didn't even turn and look at me. She just let out a hiss of smoke and went, "Biff who?"

chapter 3

Compensation

1) Payment for work performed or 2) the amount received, usually from an insurance company, to "make one whole" after an injury or loss.

"I gotta get Biff and Andy back together again."

Kendall got off his board and looked at me. He scratched his neck. All he'd ever heard me do was complain about the guy, and now here I was all desperate for Biff to come back. Kendall must have thought I was crazy, but scratching his neck in a thoughtful sort of way was about as close as he'd ever come to mentioning that kind of thing.

He just went, "Oh, yeah? They broke up? What happened?"

I thought of Andy standing there at the sink, and the way the red blotches started spreading around her eyes as if someone had just dumped a package of cherry Kool-Aid into a jug of milk. I thought of the way her chin quivered and how mean her mouth looked and the big pile of cigarettes she'd already smoked down to little crumpled butts by eight in the morning.

I thought about Kendall saying how he liked Eddie because at least Eddie made his mother happy. I realized what a jerk I used to be to Biff and what a moron I was for resenting him even though Andy had never had another boyfriend the whole time I was growing up. Not because there weren't guys who were interested—even I could see there were—but just because she didn't want me to go through the whole Dad-of-the-Month Club thing. She didn't want me to get attached to someone if she wasn't sure it would last. For fifteen years she did nothing but be my mother, and then some guy comes along—some perfectly nice guy—and I can't even say, "Good for you, have fun."

"I don't know," I said. "I don't know what happened."

But I did know. Or at least I thought I did. Andy wouldn't tell me what was up that morning, but I was pretty sure it had to do with that stupid long board.

I had this feeling, this I-ate-something-rotten feeling, that it was all my fault.

I *knew* Andy hated it when someone butted into our family business. I knew how mad she could get, how unreasonable she could be, how she could just go totally berserk at the least little thing and never, ever get over it. Didn't matter. I still made Biff swear he'd ask her about buying me that board.

My exact words: "And don't come back empty-handed. I mean it, Biff!"

I was only joking—sort of. I was only joking too when I said I wouldn't help with the meal unless he promised to get it for me. But everybody knows a lot of jokes aren't meant to be funny. Biff knew I was telling him I wanted that board, and I wanted it now.

Who cared about a stupid board? Who cared that Andy owed it to me? Who cared that she broke her promise? I mean, it's not like that was the first time she ever broke a promise.

Big deal.

When you think about it, I got paid plenty for that stupid factum. I had to stay inside one night—one night!—and do a couple hours' work so that Andy, for the first time in fifteen years, could actually go out with a guy. And look what I got for it: Andy was happy. She stopped bugging me about stuff. She hardly ever swore. She quit smoking. She laughed all the time. She cut way back on the black eyeliner. The apartment was clean. There was food on the table.

Like, what more did I want?

For the first time in my life, we were almost normal. I wanted that way more than I wanted a new board.

Kendall went, "It's probably nothing. Mom and Eddie broke up once too. They'll get over it. I bet they're back together again already."

Easy for him to say. He didn't know Andy the way I do. He didn't hear her that morning. I mean, I thought she was joking at first with that whole "Biff who?" thing.

I went, "Ahhhhhh…Biff Fougere? You know, your boyfriend? The love of your life?" She spun around like I just said rich people deserve to rule the world or something. She was panting and her bottom teeth were all stuck out at me. It was like Andy's evil twin was back again or something. She went, "Don't ever mention. That name. To me. Again."

I knew right away this wasn't some joke. She was serious. She wiped her mouth with the back of her hand and said, "He's gone. He's out of here. Good riddance! Believe me, we're better off without that *beeping* guy." She tried to smile, but she couldn't pull it off. It was like a corpse smiling or something. It was scary. It looked like it hurt.

I went, "C'mon! Like, what are you talking about? Better off without Biff? No, we aren't! We need Biff! Who's going to cook? Who's going to…"

I stopped. I wanted to come up with something really, really convincing that would make Andy go, "Oh, yeah, sorry. What was I thinking? I'll ask Biff to come back right now."

But all I could think of was that time I forgot to bring my homework to school, and Juliana Karlsen came into class and said, "There's someone in the foyer for you, Cyril. I think it's your dad." I didn't tell her any different. I just said, "Yeah, thanks" and walked down the hall like I was sporting a brand-new pair of Nikes.

I wasn't stupid enough to say something like that to Andy. Not the way she was looking at me then. It was like she was a hyena on the Discovery Channel and I was some nice rotting wildebeest carcass. She attacked. She didn't actually tear my limbs from my body, but it probably wouldn't have felt any worse if she had.

She went, "You think he's such a great guy, do you? *Do you?* Well, just goes to show what you know! You don't understand. You don't understand anything, Cyril! You think he's Dudley Do-Right. All big and strong and looking out for the little guy and everything. Well, I got news for you, Buster. You're way off. That's just an act. The truth is he—"

She stopped dead. She stood there staring at me, breathing hard, chewing on her lip, watching something play out in her brain. I was bracing for the next big blast, but it didn't come. She just yanked her head up like she was trying to get some really irritating fly off her face and turned away from me again. Her voice was quieter, but she sounded just as mad. "Forget about him," she said. "Just forget you even met the *beeping beep*. We'll be fine. Better than fine! We'll be great." She dragged so hard on her cigarette it squeaked in pain.

There was no way Andy and Biff were back together again. That much I knew for sure. Kendall was wrong.

I shrugged. "Yeah. You could be right," I said. "Wanna go down to the bowl?"

chapter 10

Non sequitur (Latin)
Literally, "It does not follow." A statement
that is the result of faulty logic.

Maybe if life had just gone back to the way it always
used to be before Biff showed up, I could have
stood it. Take-out food wasn't that bad. The mess
in the apartment had never bothered me until he started
cleaning it up. Andy'd always been a nutcase, but at least
before—when it had just been the two of us—she could occasionally be an amusing nutcase. She could still laugh at stuff
and do totally goofy, irresponsible things and say, "Who the
beep cares? We're having fun, aren't we?" Other kids' parents
didn't do that. That was at least one good thing about having
a former juvenile offender for a mother.

But life didn't go back to the way it used to be. It was as if
the more Andy said, "Forget about Biff!" the harder it was to
do. She acted like making a big point of not sitting on the love
seat he gave us would be enough to make him disappear. In
fact, it only made it worse. Trying to get comfortable in a leaky,
secondhand, beanbag chair when there was a perfectly good love
seat sitting there empty was proof positive that we'd never be
normal, that whenever we got even halfway close, we'd go and
do something to totally screw it up, to totally blow our cover.

It was like "Why even bother?" We were doomed.

I didn't know how long I could stand it. Somehow I had to get Biff back.

In the meantime, I tried to just keep my head down and avoid Andy as much as possible. I didn't want to do anything to set her off. Why is it that when other mothers get sad, they cry? When Andy gets sad, she gets mad. She was at me all the time about my homework, about hanging out at the bowl, about doing my share of the chores.

My "share" of the chores.

Like, right.

My 114 percent of them, that is.

Andy wasn't doing anything anymore, at least not around the apartment. She'd get back from work at about seven with some greasy bag of take-out, dump her stuff in the hall and start working on that stupid malicious prosecution case again. The worst part was that she usually had Chuck with her too.

I was supposed to pick up after her, do the laundry, do the dishes, take out the garbage and just generally run around getting her anything her little heart, little belly or little black lungs desired. I didn't mind the occasional trip to the law library—I was used to that at least. I'd been doing that for her for years. But I swear if I had to run down to Toulany's once more to buy Chuck a "thoda," I was going to scream. I mean, let him get his own pop! What was I—his servant or something? For some "timid" guy from backwoods Nova Scotia, he sure took to running the world pretty fast.

I'd kick the lampposts the whole way to the store and back. I couldn't believe how bad I'd messed things up this time! I'd gone and traded in a nice normal guy who actually cooked and cleaned and looked after us for some slob who treated me like I was his house elf. I mean, come on! I didn't owe Chuck Dunkirk anything. He never tried to save *my* life.

I would have loved to say something to him, but I couldn't. Andy would have totally lost it. All she could think of now was winning that stupid case. She kept on saying, "Just you wait! You'll see, Cyril. This lawsuit will be worth millions! We'll win and then we won't have to worry about money anymore. I'll buy us a nice little house somewhere in the North End. We'll take a trip maybe, buy a new TV, a computer, another round of milkshakes—whatever we damn well feel like. The sky's the limit! I'll even buy you that stupid long board since you seem to want it so bad…"

She made it sound like this was all about the money, but it wasn't. It wasn't about justice either, at least not justice for Chuck. If anything, it was about justice for Andy. I got this weird feeling she was working so hard on the case just to get back at Biff. It was as if she thought winning it was going to make him really sorry for walking away from her, for losing her, for doing whatever it was that he did to her. It didn't make any sense, but that's how I knew I was right. Andy never made any sense.

The whole thing was nuts, but what could I do? If she needed me to buy Chuck a "thoda," I bought him a "thoda." It wasn't all bad. For one thing, it got me out of the apartment for a while.

For two, it's how I caught Biff.

chapter 11

Summons

The document used by the police to compel an accused
to attend court to answer charges against him or her.

I was on my way to Toulany's for Chuck's pop. I took the
back door. I didn't usually go that way, but it was the
nearest exit, and I had to get out fast. I was desperate for
fresh air. These days, Andy was smoking like a wet log at a
Boy Scout campfire.

Chuck was producing his share of hot air too. If I had to
listen to him say, "Now, I'm juth a thimple boy from backwoodth Nova Thcothia…" once more, I was going to scream.
Who did he think he was kidding? The guy was a major Mr.
Know-it-all. He'd act all humble and then argue with Andy
as if he actually knew more about the law than she did. I don't
know why she took that crap from him.

I had to escape.

I pushed the garbage cans out of the way and stepped
into the parking lot. I heard a sound—a crunching sound,
as if someone just stomped on a cheap toy or a small
chicken or something. It made me jump. I'm not as wimpy
as that sounds. You never know what kind of stuff could be
going on behind our apartment. You hear something back
there, you jump. Even the tough guys jump. I flicked my

head around just in time to see a leg disappear down the side of the building.

It was sort of dark and everything, and I only saw it for a second, but it didn't matter. I knew it was Biff. I distinctly saw the crease in his jeans. I distinctly smelled his cologne.

I didn't think anything of it. It didn't seem creepy to me or anything. Like, *au contraire*. I was happy. I mean, Biff was back!

I started thinking, Here's my chance. I can talk to him, reason with him, work this thing out.

I ran around to the front of the building to try and catch him. I went, "Hey, Biff!" He was across the road by now, walking away from me down a side street. I screamed, "Biff!" again and ran after him.

I called him three times. I had to grab him by the arm before he finally turned around.

He acted all surprised. He went, "Oh, hey, Sport. What's up?"

I'm like, "What's up with me?! What's up with *you*? I saw you behind the apartment. I called to you. How come you didn't answer?"

He went, "Behind your apartment? Nope." He frowned. "That's weird. Wasn't me. I wouldn't have any reason to be behind your apartment. I'm just down in the neighborhood to…um…issue a, you know, summons." He couldn't even look me in the face. He squinted up at the street signs. "I should know this—but how do I get to Gerrish Lane from here?"

I just stood there and stared at him for a while. The guy was lying to me. I knew it. That was absolutely, positively his leg. Nobody around here irons their jeans. Nobody around here wears that much cologne either, unless you're counting the old lady down the street with the big hair and the souped-up walker, but I somehow doubted that "Grizzly" was her signature fragrance.

I didn't know what to say. I didn't want to accuse him of anything. I didn't want to make things any more awkward between us than they already were.

I finally just went, "It's the next left. There's the old auto body shop at the corner. You know. *Gerrish* Auto Body. You used to walk by it every day on your way back from court..."

"Oh, right. Sure. Of course! Don't know what I was thinking. Thanks," he said. He nodded and took a couple of steps away. I thought he was leaving—maybe he did too—but then he turned around and put his hand on my shoulder.

He looked terrible. He had big black circles under his eyes. He hadn't shaved in days. Even the little Velcro pad of hair he had on his head managed to look messy. All he needed was plaid pajamas and fidgety cartoon lines squiggling around his head and he'd look exactly like the "before" picture in a sleeping pill commercial. It made me think this breakup had been as hard on him as it was on us.

He said, "You taking care of yourself, Sport? Your mom okay?"

Here was my big opportunity to make my case, but I didn't know what to do with it. Should I tell him things had completely fallen apart? That I hadn't had a vegetable in weeks? That there was mold growing in the laundry hamper?

That Andy was really, really sad?

Should I tell him to call? Drop over some time? Would that just make it worse? Should I beg him to come back and fix this mess?

Or should I just butt out?

It's not like I knew what was going to work. It's not like I had any magic formula to deal with Andy either. Who did? The only thing I could think of that might work on her were tranquilizer darts, but I doubted they were legal.

Part of me just wanted to grab Biff and drag him back to the apartment and go, "Okay, you guys. Would you just start acting like grown-ups? Can we all just go back to living like normal human beings? Is that too much to ask?"

Instead I went, "Yeah. Sure. We're doing okay."

He nodded. "Good. Glad to hear it. See you soon, Sport."

That's what he said. I really, really hoped he meant it.

chapter 12

Loitering

To linger or hang around in a public place or business where one has no particular or legal purpose. In some jurisdictions, there are statutes against loitering by which the police can arrest someone who refuses to "move along."

I could have sworn I saw Biff the next night too.

I'd talked Kendall into going to the library with me. Because of all the crap going on at home, I was seriously behind at school. Ms. Cavanaugh had assigned a new video project a couple of weeks ago. I hadn't even started it. I needed to come up with an idea for it—like, right away—or I was pooched.

We'd just left the apartment. We were about half a block away when I realized I'd forgotten to bring a book I was supposed to return. I conked myself in the head and swung back around to get it.

I saw something. It was just out of the corner of my eye, but I saw it. A flash, a flicker, someone darting back into the dark. I tried to see who it was. I did this sort of Egyptian dance thing with my neck to get a better look down the street, but I was too late. Biff—if it was Biff—was gone. I might have smelled his cologne again or I might have just imagined it.

It sort of freaked me out. I went, "Did you see that?"

Kendall went, "What?"

I went, "That! Someone just, like, ducked down the street!"

I dragged him over to the side of our building and pointed.

At nothing.

There was no one there, nothing moving, no sound except us breathing. It was like a photograph of an empty street or something. Kendall raised his eyebrows and looked at me. "Okay. Is this a joke?"

"No, I saw something! Really!" I was going to say I saw Biff, but I couldn't be sure it was Biff, and even if it was, I don't know, I didn't want to talk to Kendall about that stuff. I didn't want to, like, betray Biff if it wasn't him, and I didn't want to—this sounds stupid—make it seem like I was all broken up or anything just because Biff wasn't around anymore. It's not as if he was my dad. He was just some guy.

Just some guy who actually made my mother happy. Just some guy who almost made us look normal.

Kendall must have noticed something going on behind my face. I could tell he was trying to, I don't know, reassure me. He didn't bug me about it or anything. He just said, "Coulda been a cat."

I went, "Yeah, I guess," and let it drop. It was kind of a relief. I didn't want to get sucked back into that Andy and Biff thing right then. I didn't want to wonder if I should run after him or act like nothing happened. I didn't want to wonder what Biff was doing hanging around our place again. And I didn't want to wonder why he'd pretended he wasn't. There were going to be at least one or two answers to those questions that I didn't like.

Personally, I'd rather just do my homework. At least when your answers suck there, the worst that can happen is a bad mark.

I went home, got the book and we headed back to the library.

The place was practically empty. We got on a computer right away. That was good. There's nothing like the Internet to crowd everything else out of your brain. Biff totally disappeared.

Kendall and I began to just sort of randomly Google stuff. I was looking for inspiration. I needed to find something good to do my project on.

It started off serious. We looked up stuff like "the fishing industry," "mini basketball" and "the Lebanese community in Halifax," but then it just got stupid. We went from "people who look like their dogs" to "people who look like their ferrets" to "fudge sculptures." I don't know where that came from or why fudge sculptures seemed so funny to us, but it did. We were practically peeing ourselves laughing when the librarian went "Shhhhhh!" and did the big "Boys, you know the rules" thing.

I looked up to say sorry. That's when I saw Shannondoah Boswick-Sanderson.

chapter 13

Arrest

The taking or keeping of a person in custody by legal authority, especially in response to a criminal charge.

She was standing right beside the librarian, but it took me a second to realize who she was. I mean, who'd have thought Shannondoah Sanderson would still be in Halifax? The trial was over ages ago. Why would she bother sticking around a place like this when she could be home in Los Angeles with her money and all that sun?

She looked good but not as good as she had on TV. She still looked sort of like a Barbie doll—really tall and slim and blond and everything—but now it was sort of Barbie on a bad day. The New Common Cold Barbie or something. She looked really pale and worn out, like she was just dragging herself around. The only reason I recognized her at all was that long yellow hair of hers. It almost didn't look real. (I don't think you can even buy hair like that in Halifax.)

As soon as I realized who she was, I dove under the computer desk as if someone had thrown a bomb at me. Kendall was like, "What are you doing? What's with you?"

I went "shut up!" with my eyes and wheeled his chair in front of me so I was completely hidden.

Kendall made this quiet sigh and looked straight ahead. The way he was acting, you'd swear I was always pulling stuff like this. He mumbled down his sleeve at me. "I don't get you. We were only laughing. You think the librarian's going to arrest you or something?"

I whispered, "No, it's not that! Look. Look who he's talking to!"

Kendall turned his head around and looked. I dug my nails into his leg.

I went, "Not now! What's the matter with you! She'll see."

Kendall squeezed his foot down on my thigh until I let go.

"Okay. Who is it?" he said without moving his lips.

"Ernest Sanderson's widow!"

He scrolled down the screen. He talked in a flat, low voice as if he was just trying to figure something out. "The dead rich guy, you mean?"

"Yeah."

"So? Why are you hiding then?"

I hissed up at him, "I don't want her to recognize me!"

"Why would she recognize you?" Kendall's not usually that dense. It was annoying me. I would have bitten his ankle only I'd seen what his shoes could do.

I went, "Andy was Chuck's lawyer!" before I realized that, duh, of course Shannondoah wouldn't recognize me. I never went to the courthouse.

I'd gotten all worked up about nothing. I almost laughed. I pushed Kendall away and climbed out from under the computer desk. What a dork. I mean, even if Shannondoah had recognized me, big deal. So she doesn't like my mother.

What was she going to do—attack me? My guess was she'd be too worried about breaking her nails to do something like that.

She was talking to the librarian. "No kidding! Wow. Sea lice aren't fish? I always thought they were fish. No wonder I couldn't find anything about them in that big old fish book!"

I rolled my eyes and whispered, "Can you believe her? She doesn't even know what a sea louse is!"

Kendall went, "Do you?"

I waggled my neck around. "No, but that's beside the point. *I* wasn't married to a sea louse expert. I mean, she sat all through that trial! You'd think she'd at least know what her husband was working on when he died."

I love scoring points (I'm Andy's son after all), but that's not why I suddenly went, "Yes!" It just hit me. Forget about doing a video on the fudge sculpture craze taking over the nation! I should do my project on the life—and, even better, death—of Ernest Sanderson.

I don't know why I hadn't thought of it before. It was going to be so easy. I had the inside scoop on the trial. I could fluff it up with a big long interview of Andy and Chuck talking about the case. It would be done in no time.

Kendall argued that fudge sculptures were probably more my style, but he agreed that it made sense. The Ernest Sanderson idea would win me way more points with the teacher.

I was starting to get kind of excited about this. I couldn't help thinking it was going to be good. This story had everything—money, fame, manslaughter, not to mention, of course, Miss Gingivitis USA. You couldn't make this stuff up.

I waited until Shannondoah left—I didn't want her knowing what I was up to—then I Googled Ernest Sanderson.

There was tons of stuff on the trial I could use. Now all I needed was some footage of the guy while he was alive.

We scrolled down the screen and found a TV documentary someone did a few years back called *Gleamoccino: The Story Behind the Smile*. I clicked it open.

Boy. Was Ernest Sanderson ever old. You hear about him getting all those speeding tickets on Spring Garden Road, and you see Shannondoah, and you figure he had to be sort of halfway young anyway.

Wrong.

The guy was ancient. His hair was black and his teeth—of course—were fry-your-eyeballs-out white, but he wasn't fooling anybody. He must have been at least sixty when the video was made.

The interviewer talked to him about all the cars he owned and the charities he supported and his "lovely young wife." Then they got on to the whole Gleamoccino thing. I'd seen people walking around with those white and silver coffee cups for a long time, but I'd never heard how the stuff got invented.

The show did a fast cut to this huge blowup photo of a sea louse. It looked so big and ugly and hairy we both sort of screamed. The librarian gave us his "This is your last chance" look. The announcer had one of those home-baked-goodness type voices. The way he was talking about "the tiny crustacean," you couldn't help but feel like running out and adopting one—or at least putting some money away for its college education.

After that, the show moved on to old footage of Sanderson working in a lab. It was just some university promotional video about Sanderson, this guy named Dr. Michael Reith and "their fascinating work on sea louse mating rituals." (What is it about adults? Is there some hormone or enzyme or brain rot that kicks in at some point and makes people actually start thinking things like sea lice are "fascinating"? Are scientists looking for a cure? Will it come in time for me?)

The university footage was so bad it was hilarious. It must have been done about twenty years ago, before Dr. Sanderson had his Hollywood makeover and everything. His hair was still gray and so were his teeth. Everyone in the lab looked like they were ready to go out on Halloween. They all wore pants that came up to their armpits, and glasses with lenses roughly the size of Big Macs. You'd swear they were all auditioning for the next big Pixar cartoon or something.

The thing that cracked me up, though, was this tall skinny guy with a bad disco mustache who somehow managed to weasel his way into every shot. It wasn't like the kids on TV who jump around, waving and laughing, behind the reporter when the school gets firebombed or anything. This guy was acting like he just happened to be there. The cameraman was obviously trying to avoid him, but Disco 'Stache kept edging his way back into the shot, adjusting his glasses, trying to look all Mr. Nobel-Prize-Winning Scientist and everything. You just had to laugh. The guy obviously didn't get enough attention as a child.

The rest of the show wasn't as funny, but it was pretty interesting.

According to the video, Gleamoccino started as some stupid little accident. Dr. Sanderson and the Reith guy were in the lab one day, doing their usual sea louse stuff (whatever that was). Ernie was rushing around with a pile of bugs on a tray and didn't realize he'd accidentally dropped a few of his "specimens" in Dr. Reith's coffee. (Suddenly Chuck's pumpkin boogers didn't sound all that bad to me.)

Dr. Reith noticed a sort of weird taste but didn't think anything of it until he got to the bottom of the cup and saw all these wiggly things flopping around and no doubt going, "Help me! Help me!"

He screamed. (Surprise. Surprise.)

Sanderson was all horrified at what happened. Or he was for a while anyway, until he saw how white Dr. Reith's teeth had gotten all of a sudden.

Coffee that bleaches your teeth?

These guys were no fools. They knew right away they were sitting on a gold mine.

First, though, they had to get rid of that "lousy" taste, not to mention the tooth decay, bad breath and all the other lovely side effects that early versions of Gleamoccino caused. They even had to design a stronger coffee cup because Gleamoccino whitened a hole clear through the regular ones.

It took them years, but Sanderson and Reith finally invented a "flavor-free sea louse additive" that didn't maim, mutilate or make you smell funny. They were millionaires within a few years, billionaires before you could say, "Smile for the birdie!"

Unfortunately, Mike Reith died of a degenerative nerve disease and was unable to "enjoy the full success of Gleamoccino." Ernest did his best to look really broken up when he said that—the camera even zoomed in on this one big tear just sort of glistening in his eye—but he pulled himself together enough to take viewers on a tour of his fabulous seventeen-bedroom oceanfront "cottage."

The rest of the show was about the global impact of "the world's favorite coffee." There were street shots of people drinking the stuff in front of the Eiffel Tower and Machu Picchu and the Great Wall of China and then this really depressing picture of all these white and silver cups littering the trail all the way up to the top of Mount Kilimanjaro. (Yup. Gleamoccino sure has had a global impact.)

There was so much great stuff here. I started fantasizing about my little student documentary turning into *The Inconvenient Truth about Coffee*. I could just see myself up on the podium thanking Andy, Chuck and, of course, Mary Mulderry-MacIsaac for all her love and support. I'd invite Biff to the premiere, and Andy would be so happy and proud of me that she'd actually consent to talk to him, and of course, as soon as she did, they'd both realize their mistake and they'd make up and we'd live happily ever after again.

The sad thing is I'm not joking. I actually kind of believed that.

chapter 14

Victim Impact Statement

A written statement that describes the harm suffered by the victim of an offence. It allows victims to participate in the sentencing of the offender by explaining how the crime has affected them.

The next day I made a rough cut of some of the old footage and brought it home to show Andy. I was pretty proud of it. It wasn't perfect or anything, but I figured it had to be a bit more interesting than most kids' projects. I mean, Erin Carroll was doing hers on "Advances in Carpet Cleaning: The Steam Revolution." Next to that, my little video looked like the Lord of the Rings trilogy.

Andy, of course, thought it was fabulous, but I knew she would. She's not so great about the cooking/cleaning/acting normal part of parenthood, but for a social misfit she sure is supportive. Even if I'd been the one stuck with carpet cleaning and Erin got to do Gleamoccino, Andy would have liked my project better. Being biased isn't always such a bad thing.

She wanted to borrow the camera so she could show the video to Atula and Chuck (and, no doubt, Spielberg if she could reach him), but I said no way.

She was outraged. She was like, "How come?"

I said, "What do you think I am? Crazy? I'm not giving you my project a week before it's due! You'd lose it. You're always losing stuff."

She went, "Oh, yeah? Like what?"

I rolled my eyes so far back in my head I could see my shoulder blades twitch. I went, "Please! In the last week or so, you've lost your keys, your jacket, your right boot, the Iqbal file, the groceries, your molar—I don't know how anybody can lose a tooth and not notice till they get home but, like, whatever—your earrings, your nose ring, your toothbrush, your—"

Andy sucked in her breath and punched herself in the forehead. "Oh, *beep*! That reminds me. I can't find the victim impact statement Chuck wrote. You're going to have to run over to his place and get another copy for me."

I was like, aargh! There were so many things I could say. I could bring up the obvious: that this was irrefutable proof she loses stuff all the time.

I could argue about why I should be the one to run over and pick it up. I mean, come on! *She* was the one who lost it.

I could tell her I had work to do, and, believe me, I wouldn't be lying. My project was nowhere near finished.

But I didn't say anything. Andy had laughed at the Disco 'Stache guy in the video. That was the first time she'd laughed in weeks. For a second there, it almost seemed like she was back to her old self. I didn't want to go and blow it.

I sighed. I said, "Okay. But call Chuck and tell him I'm coming. I don't want to have to wait around while he goes looking for it." I didn't really care if I had to wait around or not. I just didn't want to act too easy to get along with or Andy'd know right away I was just doing it to jolly her up. That would remind her of Biff and why she was sad in the first place. And that would make her even crankier than she was before.

Chuck lived in the basement apartment of a building even worse than ours. The carpet in the halls was the color of wet sidewalk except where it was flipping up at the edges and you could see that it had actually been pink once upon a time. People had scrawled stuff on the walls that Andy wouldn't even say to a rich guy in her worst mood. The whole place smelled like a cross between broccoli and a sick dog. I wanted to get out of there as fast as possible. It was the type of place that could sort of follow you home if you weren't careful.

There was no C. Dunkirk listed on the doorbells, but the security door was propped open, so I let myself in and went straight down to apartment 1B. I knocked. I could hear music, so I knew someone was there, but no one came to the door. I knocked again.

Chuck, like, barked out, "Who is it?" He didn't swear or anything, but you knew he was thinking of it. I mean, the guy sounded like one of the trolls under the bridge or something. Good thing I didn't bring my billy goat with me.

I went, "It's me—Cyril. I'm here to pick up your victim impact statement."

Chuck pulled the door open an inch or two, but he left the chain on. It was like he didn't trust me or something. He looked out at me with one squinted-up eye.

He went, "What? I gave that to Andy already."

I sighed. I should have known. "She can't find it. Didn't she call and tell you I was coming?"

I could tell he was pissed.

"She didn't." That was all he said. No "Why don't you come in and make yourself comfortable while I look for my copy?" No "I'd be delighted. I've spent so much time at your house, hogging the love seat and eating all the good food, it's the least I can do." There was none of that.

He just stood there staring at me like I was personally responsible for the rise in youth violence or something.

I went, "She needs another copy."

He went, "She needs it right now?"

"Yeah, right now," I said. I didn't know if that was true or not but, hey, if I can hop out and get a "thoda" for him, he can hop out and get a victim impact statement for me.

I didn't move. He didn't move. It was the classic stand-off. If he was hoping I'd succumb to the dying dog fumes, he was out of luck. He tugged at his beard. He licked his finger and pushed up his glasses. He cranked his head sideways and made his neck bones crack. He stared at me the whole time. Didn't matter. I wasn't going anywhere.

He finally caved. He made this noise in his throat. It wasn't a happy noise. If I hadn't known better, I would have thought he was having engine trouble. "Okay," he went. "Stay there. I'll get it."

"Thank you," I said and smiled. It's easy to smile when you've won.

He kept me waiting for a good five minutes. It was irritating, but it gave me a chance to snoop at his apartment. He'd left the door open a crack. I don't know if he just forgot to slam it in my face or if this was his way of being neighborly.

All I could think was: some janitor. I don't mind a bit of a mess, but his living room looked like a cross between the city dump and Andy's bedroom. There were pizza boxes all over the place, as if some kid just had a big birthday party. Newspapers and books and I don't know what else were stacked up everywhere—on the floor, on the couch, on the windowsills. It looked like he just dropped his jacket on the floor as soon as he came in the door. (What was he? Fifteen or something?)

The thing that got me the most, though, was this big picture of Ernest Sanderson tacked on the wall. (It must have been taken before he got rich because he still looked old.) I couldn't help thinking that if I'd gone through what Chuck went through with that trial, I wouldn't want to see Sanderson's face ever again.

Chuck came out of the back room and caught me sort of peering through the door. He beetled right over and blocked my view. He handed me the victim impact statement. He must have had to write it all over again. I don't know why else it would have taken him so long. He shoved it at me.

"Here," he said. "Make sure you tell your mother to call me before she sends you over again."

I said, "Don't worry. I will," but I doubt he heard. He'd already closed the door and clicked all the locks shut.

I felt weird the whole way home. Something was bugging me about my little visit with Chuck. It wasn't just that he was rude. Lots of adults are like that. They're all nice when your parents are around, then treat you like shower scum when they get you alone.

This was something else. Something didn't feel right. It was like one of those puzzles on the kiddy page where you have to spot "What's wrong with this picture?" Was it something about Chuck? Was it his gross apartment building? Was it that photo of Ernest Sanderson on the wall?

Or was it something else? I didn't know. Just thinking about it creeped me out. I suddenly got this feeling someone was following me. I kept turning around but no one was there.

Maybe it was something Chuck said.

I went through everything in my head. It didn't take me long. He hadn't said much and he hadn't said anything that stood out.

Then I thought maybe it wasn't *what* he said but *how* he said it.

I rewound the scene and played it in my head again. I pictured Chuck, staring at me through the door, licking his finger, pushing up his glasses, cracking his neck. "Stay there," he said.

"Stay there."

Sssssssssstay.

Sss.

It hit me. That was it.

Chuck Dunkirk had a full set of teeth.

chapter 15

Proof

The establishment of a fact by the use of evidence.
Anything that can make a person believe that
a fact or proposition is true or false.

Kendall was at his dad's that night, so I didn't see him until the next day. He didn't understand why I was so wound up. He acted like it was nothing. He didn't even get off his board.

"Yeah. Okay. So Chuck got a new set of teeth. Shouldn't you be happy? Think of it this way. At least he won't be spraying you with food anymore."

I went, "Yeah but…" I stopped. The problem was, I didn't have a "but." Not a real "but" anyway (or a real butt either, but that's a different story). Nothing I could put into words at least. Just this weird feeling that there was something funny about those teeth.

I got this flash of Chuck, standing at the door, clearing his throat, glaring at me. I couldn't help thinking he was up to something. It wasn't just the teeth. Why else wouldn't he let me in? Why did he immediately block my view like that? It was like he was hiding something…

Or maybe some*one*…

Don't tell me the guy had a hot date there with him! I just had to shake that idea out of my head. My stomach could only take so much. Frankly, I'd rather clean the compost bin.

It dawned on me—I hate it when this happens—that I might be nuts. Maybe Kendall was right. Maybe Chuck just got a new set of chompers.

And maybe he just didn't want me to come in because he was ashamed of the mess. Even I would have been sort of embarrassed, what with those greasy pizza boxes all over the place. I mean, that's how you get roaches. Even Andy and I don't leave food around. (Anymore, that is.)

And maybe he felt bad because he couldn't afford...

I stopped.

Pizza.

"No!" I went. I ran down into the center of the bowl and screamed at Kendall, "That's just it! The teeth aren't new. The guy had pizza boxes all over his place!"

Kendall whipped past me, did a pop shove-it and rolled back. "So? What does that prove?"

I threw up my hands. It was so obvious. "The guy can barely gum his way through mashed potatoes! How could he eat pizza with no teeth? *Railroader's* Pizza—'with its famous choo-choo-chewy crust'! Don't you watch the commercials? You practically have to be a raptor to get through one of those things."

That wasn't convincing Kendall either, but at least it made him stop. "I don't know. Maybe Chuck doesn't eat the crust. Lots of people don't eat the crust. Or maybe he uses a knife and fork. You know, cuts it up into little bite-size pieces?"

"Yeah," I went. "Or maybe he throws the whole thing in the blender and makes himself a nice little anchovy smoothie to start the day. I mean, he could. It's not impossible."

I bugged out my eyes and gave this big sigh, but only because I knew everything Kendall said made sense and I just didn't want to admit it.

You can't really hate Kendall for being smart, because he doesn't make a big thing about it or anything, but I was coming sort of close. I was right. I knew it. There was something weird here. I didn't like how Kendall kept getting in the way of me figuring out what it was.

Kendall went back to working on his kickflips. Girls were starting to hover around the bowl the way they always did whenever he was doing his stuff. Normally I'd try to horn in on the action, but even the sight of Mary Mulderry-MacIsaac popping ollies wasn't interesting me that day.

I went and sat under the tree. I stared at my shoes and chewed on the inside of my cheek. All I could think about was Chuck and those teeth. I was missing something. What was it? I tried to attack the problem logically.

I thought back. Just before I came down to the bowl, Andy and I had been looking at my video again. Chuck walked in right in the middle of it. I didn't even turn around and say hi. I couldn't. I knew there was no way I could have looked at him as if everything was perfectly normal. My face would have given me away. Chuck would have known immediately that I'd seen something. He'd have known I was suspicious of him.

Andy insisted I play the CD and show Chuck what I'd done so far on my project. I said okay. It wasn't worth fighting about. Chuck crouched down behind me. We were all squished together, practically on top of each other, trying to look through the camera's little viewfinder. Andy did most of the talking—it was all along the lines of "Isn't this fabulous?

Isn't my son brilliant?"—but Chuck said something too. What?

Think.

We'd just watched the part of the video with Disco 'Stache and the Reith guy in the lab. Then I cut to Ernest explaining how he'd accidentally dropped the sea lice in the coffee. I'd spliced in a few shots of these huge black beetles I'd put in the bottom of Ms. Cavanaugh's *World's Best Teacher* mug. They were crawling all over each other like they were playing Twister: The Insect Edition or something. It was hilarious.

Andy went, "Gross!" and laughed.

Chuck didn't laugh. I remembered that. It was supposed to be funny, but I got nothing from him. He was so serious. He went, "Thath very interethting, Thyril." I could feel the spray all over my ear.

I could still feel the spray.

The spray. Of course!

I hopped on my board and chased Kendall down into the bowl. His little posse of girls had to kind of dive for their lives.

"Oh, yeah?" I went. "Then how come he wasn't wearing them today? Huh? Tell me that!"

Kendall was like, "Who wearing what?"

"Chuck. His teeth. He wasn't wearing his teeth today! If they're new, how come he's not wearing them now? How come he's not showing them off? Like, what kind of guy wears his teeth at home but not when he goes out? I mean, is that not weird to you?"

Kendall went, "Yeah, okay, I guess. That's sort of weird."

I went, "Good. Thank you. That's all I wanted."

The girls were smiling at me, but it was in that "Poor Cyril" sort of way. I had to admit it was probably a little, I don't know, peculiar to get that excited about somebody else's dentures. Didn't matter. I felt like I'd just made some major breakthrough. The girls might have thought I was crazy, but at least *I* didn't anymore.

I stopped at Toulany's on the way home for a big bag of extra-spicy barbecue chips and a liter jug of pop. It wasn't the best dinner in the world, but I figured it was probably better than what we had back at the apartment. Andy wasn't even buying very much take-out any more. The night before, she'd brought home a single-serving taco for us *to share*. I didn't like to ask myself why. I kept on hearing Atula say, "But if you *lose* the case, of course, you will get nothing!"

Nothing.

I didn't like nothing. I'd had nothing before. Nothing isn't fun. It doesn't taste good and it doesn't keep the power going or the landlord happy. It's cold and it's dark and it keeps you up at night. Even a little bit of something— anything!—is better than that.

I got back to the apartment and there was a Tupperware container sitting outside the door with a note attached.

Hi Sport,

Thought you might like a good meal for a change. (I know your mother wasn't going to make it for you!)

Biff

I had this little life-ain't-so-bad moment. Biff cares. Food shows up when you really need it. We'd survive.

I picked up the container and went into the apartment. The place was empty. Just as well. I wasn't sure I wanted

Andy catching me eating Biff's food right then—or seeing that snarky note of his.

I tore it up and stuffed it in my pocket. It depressed me. It was so un-Biff. He always seemed to take everything in his stride. He was always the one to give people a break. He was probably the only guy in North America not cheering when that fish-eyed hairstylist from Orillia got voted off the island. What was with that "I know your mother wasn't going to make it for you" crack? I really didn't need him getting mad now too. There's no way they'd ever get back together then.

I zapped the container and sat down to eat. I was pretty full after all those chips, but I was powerless to stop myself. It was a real meal. I couldn't remember the last time I had a real meal. (Wrong. I could. It was the night Biff left.) The mashed potatoes were a little lumpier than I'd expect from him, but I didn't care. They were good. So what about the note? Why shouldn't he be mad? He had feelings too.

And Chuck? So he didn't wear his teeth. What business was that of mine? Maybe he thought he looked better without them. How would I know? Weirder things have happened. I mean, Andy preferred her pantyhose with holes in them. Maybe Chuck just thought he had particularly attractive gums or something and didn't want to hide them away behind an ugly old set of teeth.

A hot meal makes you see the world kind of different.

I put my fork down and groaned. It was good, but I had eaten too much. I put the lid back on the container and hid it in the fridge behind a tub of yogurt Andy must have bought when she was in junior high. My chicken dinner would be safe there. No way she'd ever risk going back that far in the fridge. It was like a toxic waste dump back there.

I went to turn on the TV. I had to get up to do it because the stupid remote wasn't working again. Andy had probably taken the batteries for her Dictaphone or something. I was leaning down to push the power button when I just happened to glance out the window.

That's when I saw Biff again.

It was dark out, and he was more or less in the shadows, but the circle of light from the streetlamp sort of glinted off the top of his buzz cut. I knocked on the window and gave him a thumbs-up. I was just trying to say thanks without looking too sucky about it.

Biff looked up. He didn't smile or wave or anything. He just deked back into the dark like he wasn't even there.

chapter 16

Assault
Any unlawful touching of another person
without justification or excuse.

I'm terrified. The tall skinny guy with the bad 'stache is chasing me. He's going, "I told you to get me a thoda! I want a thoda!" I'm running as hard as I can to get away from him. My lungs hurt. My ribs hurt. I can barely hear him over the sound of my own breathing.

I see an alley on the far side of our building. I never noticed that alley before. I dart down it. It's dark and wet and hollow sounding. I run and I run and I run as hard as I can. I keep going until, I don't know, I suddenly realize there's only the sound of one pair of feet slapping the pavement. I can't hear the guy screaming anymore. No footsteps. No voices. No heavy breathing. Nothing. It's just me now.

He must have given up. Made the wrong turn. Tripped. Something. Whatever. I've lost him.

I'm free! I'm going to live.

I throw my head back and kind of stagger to a stop. For a second, it's almost like I'm floating, like I just won the hundred-meter crawl or something, and now I can finally just lie on my back and relax. I almost feel kind of heroic.

Life is good for about two seconds, then *bam*! This giant sea louse leaps out at me from behind some garbage can. It's got this big wet mouth and these white, white teeth that it keeps snapping at me, and my heart slams into overdrive again. I know I'm doomed, but I start running anyway. It dawns on me that I'm a lousy runner. I've always been a lousy runner. I'm always the last in gym class. I don't know how I lost the other guy. It was a total fluke.

No way am I going to outrun some giant sea louse. It's got way more legs than I do. It's using all of them. It's not going to fall. It's not going to get tired. It's so close I can feel its sick clammy breath on my ear.

I'm all ready to give up, to go, "Okay, fine. You won!" but then I see Biff. He's sort of hiding in the dark. He's motioning for me to run to him. He's going, "C'mon, Sport! You can do it! C'mon!" I put on this big burst of speed. I'm almost there. I stretch out my hand. He grabs it. He goes, "I got you!" and I think that means I'm safe, but then I look at him. He's smiling at me, but it's not a happy smile. Not a Biff smile. It's evil, like the Joker's smile on Batman or something. It makes him look even bigger than he is. I realize he meant "I got you!" as in "You're mine, sucker!"

There's no hope now. I know that. Even my body knows that. My internal organs have already started to liquefy. It's all over. Biff's big mitts are clamping down around my neck. He's still smiling. I scream.

I kept screaming even though my eyes were open. I heard Andy going, "What is it? C-C! It's me! What is it, sweetie?"

I shook my head and she sort of swam into focus. Even in the dark, I could tell she was as scared as I was. I tried to tell her not to worry, that it was just a dream, but before I could, I started barfing.

This wasn't just a mouth-and-stomach thing. This was a full-body barf. It came in these big heaves, as if somebody had me by the feet and was playing crack-the-whip with my body. I could feel the bones in my neck snapping. By the time my insides were empty, I was exhausted. I flopped back on the bed with my mouth open and my heart pounding and just stared at the ceiling. There were little white dots dancing around in the air. I figured those were blood vessels popping. Can you go blind from barfing?

Andy cleaned me up and wiped my face with a cool cloth and sort of cradled my head in her lap. She kept going, "Oh, sweetie pie. Oh, sweetie pie." It floated across my mind that, despite everything, I loved her. I was so glad she was there. She was always there. She wouldn't desert me. I could count on her. I let her run her fingers through my hair like she used to when I was little and we'd lie in bed together reading. It felt good. Right then, those five little grooves she drew on my scalp were the only part of me that didn't want to die.

She went, "It must have been something you ate. Did you eat anything weird today, C-C?"

chapter 17

Larceny
The unauthorized taking of someone's
personal property. Theft.

I couldn't face breakfast the next day, but otherwise I felt okay. I *made* myself feel okay. I had to get that project done. I couldn't think about my empty stomach or my sore throat or why, no matter what you eat, it always smells like cheese when you barf it up. I couldn't think about Chuck's teeth or the orange envelope from the power company marked *Urgent! Payment Required* or whether Biff had actually meant to poison me.

I had to make myself believe that the only thing that mattered right then was getting an A (or at least a B or even a C) in media arts.

I just needed to get one last interview with Andy and Chuck for my Gleamoccino video. A few hours to edit, a couple more for voice-over and I'd be done. I could reward myself. Go to the bowl. Watch crappy TV. Waste time.

I snapped into gear. I was all ready to go. I had my questions written out. Andy finally had her makeup on the way she liked it—i.e., too much and messy. Chuck had even agreed to be on camera again. (Since "it'th only a little thchool project." Like he was doing me a favor or something! Right. Mr. Get-Me-a-Thoda. He so owed me.)

I looked through the viewfinder and saw a little white message flashing on the screen.

No Disc.

I immediately forgot about how lucky I was to have Andy and how much I loved her and all the other garbage I thought the night before. Now I was ready to kill her.

I was like, "Okay. Where is it? What did you do with the CD? I told you not to touch the camera!"

She went, "What? What are you talking about? I didn't touch the camera, Cyril! Why would I touch your camera?"

Just to bug me. Because I told you not to. Because you couldn't keep out of trouble even if you wanted to. There were a thousand different reasons.

I just glared at her.

She put her hands up like she was a hostage negotiator and I was some deranged maniac she had to talk down. She went, "Seriously. Honestly. We looked at it with you. Then you went to the bowl. Then we went to the law library. Then I came home and went to bed. That's it! I never touched it, Cyril. I *wouldn't* touch it. Really. Seriously. Honestly."

I could feel my brain cells exploding like popcorn in the microwave. All I could think about was how much trouble I was in. I threw my head back and did this silent scream. I started tearing the place apart.

Either Andy actually understood how important this was or she was trying to cover something up, because she didn't fight back. She always fights back, no matter how wrong she is. In fact, the wronger she is, the harder she fights. It's one of her most effective defenses.

She started tearing the place apart too.

Chuck, meanwhile, was sort of doing this half-hearted attempt to look. He shuffled a few flyers around. He lifted up a cushion on the love seat but was too lazy to lean his head down low enough to actually see under it. He went, "Ith anything elth mithing?"

Andy stopped tossing around a pile of old newspapers and went, "What? Sorry. Can you say that again?"

He went, "Mithing? You know, gone. Ith anything gone?"

I felt like saying, "Would you just put your teeth in?" but I didn't. I didn't even answer. Who cared about anything else? Was anything else due Tuesday? I shook my head and sort of growled under my breath.

Andy ignored me. She looked at Chuck and went, "Why?"

Chuck licked his finger and pushed his glasses up. "I don't know. Maybe there wath a robbery and the perpetrator took the thee dee too."

Andy slapped her hand on her cheek.

"Of course! That's it, Chuck! I bet we were robbed!" She looked at me like, See! I told you I didn't do anything.

It was so stupid I couldn't even get mad. I made my face go all flat. I went, "What would anyone steal from us? We don't…have anything…worth taking."

Andy dropped her jaw and bugged her eyes out at me. She went, "Cy-ril!" all insulted and everything. "We've got lots of stuff other people would want!"

I couldn't control myself anymore. I did this spokes-model-from-hell thing with my hands. "For instance, this lovely, secondhand, twelve-inch, black-and-white television set with its matching cardboard entertainment unit—otherwise known as a box."

Andy was mouthing "ha-ha" and desperately looking around the room for something worth stealing.

I ran over to the windowsill. "Or this state-of-the-art 1976 radio–alarm clock with its unique Screeching Zombies reception system."

She went, "That works perfectly well. It's vintage. People pay a lot of money for vintage radios."

I picked her fourteen-dollar Salvation Army "fur" coat up off the floor. "Or, of course, this new-to-you designer mink, complete with bright red ketchup accent and fuzzy pocket mints!"

I threw it back down on the floor. I went, "Well, looks to me like all of our valuables are safe. So much for the robbery idea."

I tipped over the beanbag chair. I found a pair of socks I hadn't seen since grade four and about a buck in change but no CD.

Andy went, "My toe rings! They're…they're gone!"

I ignored her. I knew what she was up to. Another one of her diversionary tactics. I wasn't falling for it. I got down on my knees and looked under the love seat. The dust bunnies were breeding. Another reason we needed Biff.

I would have stayed under the love seat until the grief counselors came and took Andy away, but my asthma was starting to kick in.

I got up. Andy and Chuck were over by the window, looking all devastated. Andy was saying, "They were right here! I'm sure of it. I was sitting on the floor doing my toenails and I put them here and now…" She paused as if it was too painful to go on. "And now, they're gone!"

She got those toe rings on the street, five for two bucks. Like someone's going to break into the apartment for that. They would have been better off stealing our recycling bag.

Chuck was nodding and tapping his finger against his lips as if he was Sherlock Holmes hot on the trail of some international diamond thief or something. He went, "Hmm. Yeth. Anything elth dithappear you can think of?"

Andy scoped the room like she was some emo snowy owl looking for prey. I wanted to kill her. Why did I have to put up with this garbage?

She gasped and fell against Chuck. "My *Catcher in the Rye* is gone!"

I looked at the busted TV we use as a coffee table. Andy was right. *The Catcher in the Rye* was gone.

That might not sound like such a big deal to most people. It's this beat-up old book held together with an elastic band. You can pick up one just like it at almost any yard sale for a quarter.

But this was serious.

Andy loved that book more than anything in the world (with the possible exception of me and cigarettes, although not necessarily in that order). When she was living on the street, she used it as a pillow. When other mothers were reading *Go, Dog. Go!* to their kids, she was reading me *The Catcher in the Rye*. She liked to keep it close enough that she could flip through it whenever she needed a little hit of Holden Caulfield to make it through the day. She always kept it on that busted-up TV like it was a little shrine or something. Her friends all knew how important it was to her.

Call me crazy, but for a second there I started to think someone might have stolen some stuff after all.

Andy was sitting on the love seat, rocking back and forth, going "Holden! Holden!" like someone had just kidnapped her kid. Chuck was patting her back. I couldn't tell if he was trying to comfort her or burp her.

The CD with my entire project on it disappears, and this is what I get? What a touching scene.

I came to my senses.

I went, "Would you just quit it! It wasn't a robbery. The windows are all locked. The door wasn't kicked in. No one came in here. Why would they bother? For your rings? My video project? Some old beat-up copy of *The Catcher in the Rye*? I don't think so. That stuff isn't worth anything to anybody. It's only important to us."

For a second, Andy's lip stopped quivering and she looked like she was going to argue with me, but then her face changed. Her eyes squinted up, all mean. If she had been outside, I'm pretty sure at this point she would have spit on the ground. Instead she just turned up her nose as if something smelled bad and said, "You're right. And I bet that's *exactly* why he took it."

I didn't need to ask who she meant.

chapter 18

Circumstantial Evidence
Evidence in a trial which is not directly from an eyewitness or participant and requires some reasoning to prove a fact.

I guess that would have been the time to mention that I'd seen Biff hanging around outside the apartment. I could have told Andy how he lied about being there, how he hid when I waved at him.

But I didn't. Biff even daring to show his face in our neighborhood would be all the proof Andy needed to convict him of breaking into our apartment and robbing us blind—if stealing someone's toe rings amounts to robbing them blind, that is.

I kept my mouth shut. I still wanted to believe there was another reason for Biff to act the way he did. I mean, I sort of thought of him as my friend. You know, my buddy. Even—this is kind of embarrassing—my dad or at least my almost dad or, like, I guess, my almost stepdad or whatever.

I had to admit it didn't look all that good. I'd seen Biff skulking around. He had a key to the apartment. He wouldn't have needed to break in. He knew all about Andy's *Catcher in the Rye* obsession. He knew how much losing that book would bug her. He cleaned the apartment all the time too, so he was probably the only person who knew where she usually left her toe rings (or the nail scissors or the clean towels or the egg flipper, for that matter).

The evidence was piling up against him, no question about it, but I just couldn't believe it. I mean, Biff just didn't seem to me like the type of guy who would do something like that. I know that's what people always think. No one ever suspects. Reporters interview the little old lady who lives next door to some deranged serial killer and she always says, "Why, I can't believe it! He was such a nice man. So polite and quiet!" She never asked herself why he always seemed to be out digging holes in the backyard at 2:00 AM. She figured he was just doing a little late-night gardening, I guess.

Well, call me Myrtle, because I couldn't believe it either. Biff cleaned the compost bin! He gave us his love seat! He did lots of nice stuff for us he didn't need to do.

He made me that chicken dinner just because he knew I liked it and probably wasn't being fed all that well since he left. And okay, I did end up getting sick after I ate it, but I went to the bowl that day after school. I got home a lot later than I should have. The food had probably been sitting out in the warm hall for a while, growing bacteria or whatever, so, like, maybe it was my own fault. I bet he didn't mean to poison me.

And he probably hadn't seen me when I waved to him or heard me when I called him, and it's not that hard to forget the name of a street, even if you walk by it every day. He probably had other things on his mind.

He was a nice guy. He was.

He was.

I was almost sure of it.

chapter 15

Appeal
A process for making a formal challenge to a verdict.

I didn't need this right now. I really didn't.

I blew up. I went, "Quit dreaming, would you? Nobody stole anything! You might have time for this garbage, but I don't. I'm leaving! I've got to redo my entire stupid project thanks to…"

I shook my head. I shut my mouth. I didn't want to get into it with her right now.

I kicked the beanbag chair and stuff sprayed out as if it was choking on a mouthful of crackers.

Andy went, "Cy-ril!"

I just waved my hand at her and went, "While I'm gone, do something useful, why don't you, and clean your room! It's a pigsty."

Somebody had to be the grown-up around here.

I stormed out of the apartment. I didn't even look around to see if Biff was hiding in the bushes anywhere. I was sick of adults and their childish behavior. This was like recess at the Big Baby Daycare or something. I had one kid playing Make Believe, another one playing Hide-and-Go-Seek and another one who was having major teething trouble.

Get me out of here. Even doing homework was better than this.

I was lucky it was another slow night at the library. Hardly anyone was there. I couldn't even see a librarian. I sat down at the computer and Googled Ernest Sanderson. I was just waiting for the lab footage to come up when I heard this lady's voice go, "Ah, 'scuse me? Excuse me?"

No one answered. I tried to ignore her but she started doing that "Yoo-hoo!" thing. I figured some poor sucker's mother had just come to pick him up and/or publicly humiliate him. This I had to see. I was usually the one trying to disappear into my hoodie.

I peeked around. I didn't want to be too obvious about it. I've got a heart.

It wasn't anybody's mother. It was Shannondoah, waving and calling to someone. I looked behind me to see who it was.

There was nobody there. My face got all prickly. I swallowed. I turned back around really slowly.

Shannondoah was still waving and smiling. She said, "No, no. I mean you."

That's what I was afraid of. I pointed at my chest and went, "Me? You…um, ah…me?" I must have come across like Tarzan of the Apes or something. (Right. In my dreams. Tarzan of the Spider Monkeys was more like it.)

She nodded again, lifted her eyebrows and smiled some more. My heart bounced off the roof of my mouth and nearly gave itself a concussion. Shannondoah was really pretty when she smiled. It wasn't just her teeth—although I had to admit that Gleamoccino stuff was amazing. Her eyes sparkled too. She didn't look tired at all when she smiled.

"Sorry to bother you," she called out. "I can't find anyone to give me a hand around here, and you teenage guys all seem to know so much about computers. Could you just help me for one itty-bitty second? Please?"

Sure. Once I regain control over my limbs, I'd love to help you.

"Yeah, okay," I said. My voice came out like it belonged to Dora the Explorer or something.

I walked over all Mr. Roboto and sat down next to her. I felt like I was about five and my feet were dangling a foot off the floor. It was so weird. It was like having the world's prettiest babysitter. I couldn't even look at her.

Shannondoah grabbed the arm of my chair and pulled me toward her. "Now don't be shy! I won't bite." She smelled nice. She smelled like someone Biff would go out with.

She went, "You're going to think I'm the worst old dummy. I come into the library every day, but I still haven't got the hang of these computers."

She smiled again. I didn't think she was a dummy at all. It was weird. The more she smiled, the smarter I thought she was. Or maybe just the less I cared.

She picked up her notes and put them in a neat pile next to the computer. "Okay," she went. "Now tell me what I'm doing wrong here. I'm trying to look some stuff up, and the librarian said I had to go to this, ah, searching thing…"

"Search engine?"

"Yeah, something like that. So I just type it in…"

I didn't know how she could type with those big long nails. It was like tap-dancing on stilts or something. She looked around the keyboard for a couple of seconds, then went, "Oh! There it is!" and hit the Enter button.

"See what happens?" she said to me. Her eyes were this amazing light green, like a lime popsicle or something. "It keeps saying it can't find the site."

I looked at the screen. I was glad to have something to look at other than her. My tongue was starting to dry out.

I went, "Oh. Ah...yeah. It's, ah, like—you know—Google. com—not gargle.com."

She looked at the screen, then she looked at me, then she let out this huge laugh. (The librarian would have thrown her out for sure had he caught her.) It surprised me. She didn't look like the type that would have a huge laugh, but it totally suited her. It made me kind of laugh too.

"Oh, that's funny! *Google*, that's what he said! I couldn't figure out why the librarian wanted me to gargle sea lice. I get plenty in my coffee every day, thank you very much..."

I got up to go, but she grabbed me by the arm.

"Sorry. Can you stay for a second or two longer—just to make sure I'm doing this right?" She tilted her head and looked up at me with these big green eyes, and it was kind of corny and cheesy, but hey. It worked. Who cared about my project? I could just call this research. Maybe I'd find out something about Ernest that I could use in my video.

"Yeah, sure, okay," I went. "What else do you want to look up?" I was proud of myself. I hardly sounded like a cartoon character at all.

Shannondoah rifled through her pile of papers and found the one she was looking for.

"Okay, let's see. How about we start with Power Powder?"

I walked her through the process again. The Power Powder site was down—the company had apparently gone out of business—but there were a number of other articles on the stuff. Shannondoah didn't even know how to double click, so I stayed with her while she printed a few pages out. By the second time she did it, she seemed to know her way around. I didn't know why she thought she was dumb. She picked up the computer stuff faster than Andy, and Andy uses a computer every day.

"Why, isn't this fabulous!" she said. "It's not hard at all. It's *way* easier than rooting around through a bunch of old books. Now let me do one all by myself, okay? What do I have next on my list? Let's see…P-a-t-e-n-t. Space. P-r-o-t-e-c-t-i-o-n. Patent protection. Sounds like something you do to your shoes, doesn't it? Then just hit 'I feel lucky' and—voila!"

A legal site came on the screen. Shannondoah threw her hands up in the air. She went, "You're a genius!"

Then she leaned over and kissed me on the cheek.

I don't know what I looked like from the outside, but inside I was definitely doing the whole bug-just-slammed-into-windshield thing. I think Shannondoah must have seen that too. She let out another one of those big laughs.

She went, "You're cute!" and wiped her lipstick off my face with her thumb. "There. All gone! Don't want your girlfriend getting jealous of an old widow-lady like me!"

I sort of stumbled back to my corner. None of the guys at school were ever going to believe that Miss Gingivitis USA kissed me. Those posters they had up all over the reading room were right. *Libraries can be fun*!

I tried to concentrate on my project, but my mind (and my eyes) kept wandering. I mean, you really never know about people. For starters, who'd have thought Shannondoah Sanderson would think someone like me was cute?

And, for seconds, who'd have thought someone who looked like her would spend her time in a library? I'd been all ready to write her off as some blond bimbo when I saw her on TV, but here she was again, doing research—and it wasn't on nail polish or hair color or some celebrity's love life or anything. She was looking up Power Powder. Unless I was wrong, that was the cleaning stuff Chuck threw on the fire.

I wondered what she was up to. Was she thinking of appealing the case or something? It wouldn't be that surprising. I mean, lots of cases get appealed. If lawyers can find one tiny thing the judge did wrong or one little itty-bitty legal loophole, they'll try and get another trial—and hopefully this time a verdict they like too.

It dawned on me that I should probably tell Andy about what Shannondoah was doing and give her a chance to get prepared. That's what a good son would do.

I thought about it for a couple of seconds. My choice: Betray my mother. Or betray Miss Gingivitis USA. The answer was clear. I guess I wasn't a good son.

I put a CD in the computer and copied the footage I needed for my project.

Shannondoah stuck her hand up and waved. "Yoo-hoo! I'm going now! Thanks again!"

I smiled and waved back.

I waited for the tingling in my spine to calm down and then I tried to focus on my project again. Was there anything else I needed? I printed off some still shots that I could maybe use for a poster. Ms. Cavanaugh hadn't asked for a poster, but there could be some extra points there for me. I copied a few things on the trial too. Then I got up to go.

The fastest way out of the library was straight past the returns desk, but, I don't know why (okay, that's a lie), I went the long way, past Shannondoah's seat. Maybe this is what they mean when they say criminals always return to the scene of the crime.

I tried to make it look natural, like it was no big deal, like I just had a bad sense of direction or something.

I sort of glanced down at her desk as I went past. I guess I was half hoping to see her face reflected in the screen, smiling back at me, blowing a kiss, doing that "You're cute" thing again.

No such luck. But there was something even better there. Shannondoah had left one of her papers behind.

I picked it up and bolted out of the library.

chapter 20

Eviction

Ousting a tenant who has breached the
terms of a lease or rental agreement.

I ran up and down the street a couple of times, but
Shannondoah was long gone. I was sort of hoping I'd at
least find a glass slipper or something, but the nearest I
came was a grubby gray gym sock all balled up and perched
on the ground like a big outie bellybutton. (I didn't think it
was hers.) After a while, I just stopped, kicked a couple of
pebbles in disgust and then stuffed the piece of paper into my
pocket.

Who was I kidding? What difference would it have made
if I caught up to her? I was totally dreaming. Gus the Mouse
didn't get Cinderellie. The Prince did.

Back to reality. Back to this stupid project. I checked my
watch: 7:45 PM. The media arts lab at school was open until
nine. If I booted it, I figured I could at least throw *something*
together tonight. Better than nothing.

Mr. Yurchesyn, the technician, wasn't thrilled to see me
showing up so late, but I squeezed past him.

I sat down next to this kid everyone calls Fitzmo who
was even further behind than me. I loved sitting by that guy.
He always made me look good.

I turned on the computer. I got this sudden brain wave. Maybe I wasn't in as much trouble as I thought I was. Maybe I'd saved my project onto the hard drive here. I keyed in my password. There it was! *Chuck and Andy*. It looked like something was finally going right for me.

I clicked it open.

I let out a big sigh and clunked my head on the computer. It wasn't what I was hoping for. It was just some footage from that dinner we'd had after Andy won the case. That wasn't good for anything.

Okay. Fine. Forget it. I closed the file, put my CD in the computer and started editing my project from scratch. I was in the worst mood. That whole Shannondoah thing had kind of taken my mind off Andy for a while, but there was nothing distracting me now. Just looking at the footage made me mad. Andy was the reason I had to do the project over again. The malicious prosecution suit was the reason we were getting those orange envelopes from the power company. Chuck was the reason I could barely stand going home anymore.

Chuck.

More like Upchuck.

I couldn't stand the guy.

I really wished I was a better person. Honestly. I wished I could look at people and see what's good about them and not just kind of zoom in on their faults. The man I would someday like to be wouldn't even notice if someone was a know-it-all or a mooch or a little short on teeth.

But I'm still a kid. Call me shallow, but I find it hard to remember that somebody tried to save a person's life when he's spitting all over my dinner. I find it hard to be crazy about somebody who's making me miserable.

That part in the video where Eva Jackson "from the award-winning CJCH news team" talks about Chuck came on the screen. She said something about "the timid, uneducated man at the center of the case." I almost screamed. Timid? Please. Some investigative journalist. Eva obviously never talked to the guy. I couldn't believe she fell for that big act of his.

I stuck my hands in my pockets to keep from punching the screen. I took a couple of big breaths. I was being stupid. Why work myself up over something like this now?

I felt Shannondoah's paper in my pocket. There was one sort of nice thing in my life anyway.

I decided to give myself a little break.

I took the paper out and opened it up. Shannondoah had the kind of handwriting girls practice on their binders. All kind of neat and curlicue. I bet she'd spent hours perfecting it when she was a kid.

I was sort of hoping the note would say something like *Call me sometime, Big Boy*, but I wasn't even close. *Avenues to Explore* was written in big letters at the top of the page. Underneath was just a bunch of almost-questions.

Flammability of Lice?
Location of Fire Extinguishers?
Assistants?
Traffic Court?
Phone/E-mail Records?
Patent Protection?
Appeals?

I breezed through the list. None of it made much sense to me, but that *Appeals* thing stopped me cold.

I was right. Shannondoah must have been thinking of trying to overturn the verdict. She wanted a new trial.

My stomach clenched in that chicken-and-mashed-potatoes-left-out-in-a-warm-hall sort of way.

I wasn't blinded by her green eyes anymore. I could see what this really meant now. Andy would do the appeal on contingency too. How long could we go without money coming in? She was spending too much time already on Chuck's malicious prosecution suit. Was she doing anything for her paying clients these days? Was any money coming in? I could feel everything starting to slip away.

Andy doesn't mind when money gets tight, but I've always hated it. It's scary. Food starts getting scarce. The landlord starts pushing madder and madder letters under the door. We stop answering the phone because we don't want to talk to the guy from the power company or the collection agency or even Atula, who's wondering how she's going to pay the office expenses on her own.

Then the phone gets cut off and at least we don't have to worry about the calls anymore. The hard part then is coming up with excuses. Other kids just don't get it. They don't even know you can lose your phone service. They don't understand why we don't answer the door anymore. It's like they live in a fantasy world or something.

It's stupid, but I could feel my eyes start to sting. It didn't matter how pretty Shannondoah was or that she'd actually kissed me. Thinking about her couldn't make me forget those orange envelopes.

Mr. Yurchesyn said, "Okay, guys. Lab closes in half an hour. Start winding things up. Get focused."

Right. Get focused. Forget about feeling sorry for yourself. Do your work. I stuffed the note back in my pocket. I shook my head until things straightened up inside.

I just had to attack my project one step at a time.

1. Put in the credits.

> *From Louse to Lousy Rich: The Life and Death of Ernest Sanderson.*
> *Conceived, written, directed, videotaped and edited by Cyril F. MacIntyre*

Should I mention that I did the voice and soundtrack too? I considered it for a second, then decided against it. If I added that, I'd have to make my name smaller.

2. Arrange to take some before and after shots of kids' teeth the next day. Ask Fitzmo. His are so gray they're almost green. He's a prime Gleamoccino candidate.

3. Cut out a bit of the footage of Sanderson's early years. It doesn't add much to the story—except the idea that even hopeless nerds can some day make a lot of money and end up with Miss Gingivitis USA.

4. On second thought, don't cut it after all. We all need hope.

Mr. Yurchesyn gave the twenty-minute warning.

5. Tighten up the sequence in the lab.

That whole scene was way too long and had hardly anything at all to do with Gleamoccino. I should have just focused on Sanderson and Reith, but I couldn't resist keeping

Disco 'Stache in there. I figured I owed it to the guy. My life really, really sucked at the moment, but he made me laugh. He'd made Andy laugh. If he wanted fame, I'd give it to him.

I couldn't resist. I knew I didn't have much more than fifteen minutes left, but I hit Rewind and watched him weasel his way into the frame again. The guy was about as smooth as Mr. Bean and just as out of it.

I was looking at the footage for, like, the hundredth time, just sort of fast-forwarding through it, when I practically fell off my chair.

I couldn't believe what I was seeing. For a second there, I thought I was just imagining it. Like maybe I was tired or had spent too much time in front of the computer or something. I mean, how could I not have noticed this before?

I scrolled back and watched him do it again.

No, I wasn't losing my mind. I saw what I saw, and I knew right away where I'd seen it before.

Disco 'Stache licked his middle finger and pushed his glasses up his nose.

chapter 21

Dolus malus (Latin)
Fraud. A false representation of fact that is intended
to deceive another so that the individual will
act upon it to her or his legal injury.

W hy was I scared? What was there to be scared of?
I didn't know, but something was making my
heart go crazy. It was like a sumo wrestler was
stomping the yard in my chest or something. It was making
my teeth vibrate.

Mr. Y went, "Fifteen minutes, people!"

I had to act fast. I printed off a still photo of Disco
'Stache. I stared at it. What was I thinking? The guy was
young and skinny and had a full set of teeth. So he licked his
middle finger before he pushed his glasses up.

Big deal.

I bet he and Chuck weren't the only guys to do that. It's
not that unusual. Other people must do it too. (It wouldn't
have surprised me if they had their own website. You know,
www.fingerlickingdudes.com or something.) This was just
a coincidence. That skinny guy didn't look anything like
Chuck.

I rolled my eyes at myself. I was getting all worried about
nothing. Like I needed to waste the twelve and a half minutes
I had left over stuff like this?

I took my pen and just sort of scribbled over Disco 'Stache's face in disgust. I pushed it out of the way and turned back to the screen. Finish your project! Would you just get to work?

I tried but I couldn't concentrate. I don't know why, but I had to look at the picture again. It's like it had me hypnotized or something. Like it was going, "Cy-ril! Cy-ril! Look into my eyes. Look deep into my eyes…"

I looked.

Weird.

Not weird. Creepy.

Hair-standing-up-on-the-back-of-my-scrawny-neck type creepy.

It was just this sort of wiggly scribble of black ink, but if you squinted and turned the page a bit sideways, it kind of looked like a beard.

The sumo wrestler started in on his routine again.

It looked a lot like a beard. It looked a lot like Chuck. Not the nose really. Not the glasses. The ones he wore now weren't quite as out of style. But the eyes. The eyes hadn't changed.

No use trying to work now. I had to see if I was right.

I drew in the rest of the whiskers, blacked out the front teeth, added some bags under his eyes, Chuckified his hair.

That's when Sumo invited some of his wrestling buddies to join his routine.

My hands were shaking so bad now I could barely hit the right keys. I braced my arm against the desk and somehow managed to pull up that old footage I had of Chuck from the dinner party. I held the Disco 'Stache picture up and nudged Fitzmo.

"Hey. Quick. Does the guy in the picture look like the guy in the video to you?"

Fitzmo killed a few more aliens, then looked over. He scrunched his lips practically up to his nose and rocked his head back and forth. "Yeah," he went. "Maybe, a bit I guess. But hey! Do you know who he looks even more like?"

"No, who?" Maybe I was missing something here. Something obvious.

"Ms. Cavanaugh."

I couldn't help it. I laughed. He had a point.

Mr. Y went, "Ten more minutes, guys. Then I'm going home whether you're ready or not. Start putting your stuff away."

It wasn't a perfect match. It wasn't like the guy was a clone or anything, but there was definitely something there. Twenty years can make a big difference in a person. (Case in point: At ten, Andy sang in the church choir.) It wasn't unreasonable to think Chuck could be Disco 'Stache, but how would I know for sure? I could hardly ask him. Fingerprints wouldn't help unless I had some from both of them—and, of course, a little help from the guys at *CSI*. One way or another, I needed something to prove this wasn't just Ms. Cavanaugh on a bad day.

But what? The video was shot before I was even born. How was I ever going to find out who that guy was?

I looked at the screen. The show kept rolling. DNA matching, FBI profiling, X-ray vision. I couldn't think of anything that would help me.

Then it just hit me. I didn't need anything that fancy. I just needed the credits! Disco 'Stache might not have gotten the star billing he wanted, but the filmmakers probably thanked him, if only to make him go away and leave them alone.

Yurchesyn was doing this irritating "Tick...tick...tick" thing as if he was a bomb about to go off. (I'd seen him get mad before. It might not have been a joke.)

I opened the old Gleamoccino documentary and whizzed through the credits.

No luck. No Chuck.

I chewed on a hangnail and thought about it for a second.

The guy was a scientist. Maybe he didn't use the name Chuck. Maybe Charles sounded more, you know, scientific to him or something. (I mean, who'd have listened to a guy named Al Einstein or Izzy Newton?)

I scrolled back and replayed the credits.

Yes! There was a Charles.

· No, there wasn't.

Charles was the guy's last name, not his first. I kept going through the credits and then something—I don't know what—made me go back. It was like my eye had seen something that my brain hadn't.

I looked at the credit again. "Thanks to Ernest Sanderson, Ph.D., Michael Reith, Ph.D., and Duncan Charles from the Stanford University Sea Louse Laboratory."

Duncan Charles.

Charles Duncan.

Chuck Duncan.

Chuck Dunkirk.

Cue the drumroll. I was pretty sure it wasn't a picture of Ms. Cavanaugh now.

Mr. Y went, "Six minutes, everybody. And that means you, Cyril MacIntyre."

I shuffled some papers around with my left hand to make myself look busy and Googled Duncan Charles with my right.

Tons of hits. I doubted he was the Duncan Charles who won
the Ukelele World Speed Strumming championship or the
Dunkin' Duncan Charles who won the Oreo-eating contest at
the Quispamsis Fall Fair, but I could have been wrong. (That
belly had to have come from somewhere.)

My guess was the Duncan Charles I was looking for was
the one who wrote "The Atlantic Sea Louse: An Academic
Treatise on the Blah-Blah-Blah Great-Big-Word Whatever."
I wondered too if he was the same guy writing all the stuff on
a site called www.patentlyfalse.org. There was a whole bunch
of scientific garbage on that too.

I didn't have time to find out.

Mr. Y was heading right for me. I figured I wasn't going
to get much out of the academic paper on sea lice. (I couldn't
even understand the title.) Instead I just clicked one of the
patentlyfalse.org entries and hit Print. They were at least
shorter. I'd see what this Duncan Charles was talking about
when I got home.

Mr. Y went, "No, no, no, no, Cyril! You don't have time to
print anything."

"Oh, c'mon, Mr. Yurchesyn! It's only one page. Please."

"No, I gave you plenty of warning."

"I really, really, really need it for my project. Please?"

"No, my hockey game starts in fifteen minutes. I'm
not missing it because you didn't get organized earlier. Ms.
Cavanaugh assigned that project ages ago."

I was down on my knees doing my best "I beseech thee"
lowly peasant routine when I heard paper start fluttering
out of the printer. Mr. Y heard it too. He rolled his eyes and
yanked me up by the armpits. I got the feeling he was the
enforcer on the team.

"Okay, okay," he went. "Go get it, then get out of here!"

"Thanks, Mr. Y! You're a great guy."

I've got to give him credit. He sort of laughed. "And you're a pain in the neck."

I stuffed the page and the pictures in a file folder and headed home.

I wanted to check out my theory.

chapter 22

Eavesdropping

Listening to conversations or observing conduct which is meant to be private. Generally, the term "eavesdropping" is used when the activity is not legally authorized by a search warrant or court order. The term "surveillance" is used when the activity is permitted by law.

I was almost too late. I was coming round the corner onto our street when I saw Chuck leave our apartment building. I picked up speed.

I was just about to call out "Hey, Duncan!"—I wanted to see if he turned his head—when he started to run across the street. I was shocked. Who'd have thought a guy his size could run? It was like seeing the statue of Winston Churchill in front of the library break into a gallop or something. He went, "Thtop! Wait!" in this kind of loud whisper. Then he started yammering at someone.

Who? I couldn't see.

Was it Andy? I didn't think so. I never heard Chuck talk to Andy in that tone of voice. He was always kind of aw-shucks with her. Even when he was giving her one of his law lectures, he did it in that whole backwoods-boy way of his.

Who else could it be then? It wasn't a stranger. I don't know why I knew that, but I did. I guess you talk to a stranger differently than you talk to someone you know.

But who else did Chuck know? It's funny, but it never dawned on me before that he might actually know anybody other than us. I mean, no one showed up at court for him. No one apparently ever wanted him home in time for supper. He clearly didn't have a hairdresser. I doubted Atula was hanging around on a street corner waiting for him.

I had to see what this was about. I snuck around and crouched down behind this garbage can that had been left out in front of our apartment about two years ago. It wasn't the ideal vantage point, but it was the closest thing I could find. Chuck was blocking my view, and I couldn't hear what he was saying either, but you could just tell by the way he was sort of throwing his neck out and jerking his arms around that he was all wound up about something.

I was just about to boot it across the street to see if I could get a better look from behind a mailbox over there when Chuck suddenly turned to go. This time, I heard what he said loud and clear. He went, "Yeah. Don't you worry. I'll thee you then!"

I yanked my head back behind the garbage can like I was some cartoon turtle darting back into my shell. All I'd needed was one clear view of who he was talking to—and I'd got it.

I guess I should have known.

It was Biff Fougere.

chapter 23

Per minas (Latin)
Threatening someone with harm.

I leaned my back up flat against the garbage can and sucked in my breath. (Bad idea. Boy, did that thing stink.) This was too weird. Why was Chuck talking to Biff? Were they fighting? Was it that old jealousy thing again?

Could have been. Chuck was still spending most of his waking hours with Andy. But if it was jealousy, why was he making plans to meet Biff later? They didn't strike me as the type of guys who'd want to get together to talk about their feelings.

Maybe they were going to have a duel or something. That was totally weird but might be pretty cool too. I mean, *I'd* definitely go to watch. And I knew Fitzmo would be up for it too.

I didn't have time to figure out what was happening.

Andy barreled out of the building, going, "Chuck! Chuck! Phew! You're still here. You forgot your file. I didn't know if I should run it over to you or wait until Cyril got...Cyril?! What are you doing hiding behind the garbage can like that? How long have you been there? What are you doing? Spying on someone or something?"

There's one thing I can count on in this life and that's Andy. If I haven't managed to get myself in enough trouble, she's always there to push me in a little deeper.

I mentally scrolled through my options. I picked the best one I had. It was pathetic, but what could I do? I sort of wobbled up to my feet. I put my hand over one eye and went, "Ah, I, ah…I must have, like, slipped and knocked myself out or something. Out cold. Totally unconscious. You know. Unable to hear anything. Or see anything. Or anybody. Honest."

Andy pulled her head way back and went, "Yeah. Right. Like I'm going to fall for that. What? Did you forget I used to be a juvenile delinquent?"

That's it, Andy. Nice and loud. Make sure the neighbors all hear.

"You can't fool me. Cut the crap. You were up to something!"

Chuck stepped up to my so-called defense.

"I wouldn't be tho quick to judge, Andy." He flashed his gums in that charming way of his. "The boy may thtill be weak from the other night. I theem to remember he wath quite ill. Mind if I ekthamine him? I wath trained in firtht aid."

Andy nodded and her face went all TV-doctor on me. (Apparently, to look concerned you just have to tilt your head and raise your eyebrows in the middle. She did it amazingly well.) It didn't seem to bother her that the last time Chuck practiced his rescue skills on someone, they ended up in the morgue.

Chuck took me by the shoulder and spun me around so we were face-to-face. He yanked down my lower lid so hard you'd swear he was trying to whip a tablecloth off without knocking over the dishes. "Your pupilth look okay. No indication of a concuthion."

He clamped his hands around my head and squeezed. I felt my ears touch in the middle. "Nothing theemth to be broken."

He rubbed his hands through my hair in a way that can only be described as a "rolling power noogie."

He went, "Let thee if you got a bump here...Funny. People uthally have a bump when they knock themthelf out."

He mussed up my hair and gave me a "playful" push. "You muth juth be lucky, I gueth."

Andy suddenly realized how close she'd come to losing me. She threw her arms around my neck and went, "Oh, C-C!"

As if that wasn't bad enough, when she did it, she knocked the file out of my hands. It scattered on the ground. There was Duncan Charles looking up at us with his blacked-out teeth and scribbled-in beard. I kicked it over with my foot.

Chuck went, "Whatth that?"

I went, "Nothing. It's nothing. Just my project."

Andy went, "Nothing?! Don't be ridiculous. This isn't nothing! This is going to be the best video project Citadel High has ever seen! Trust me, Chuck. Cyril has done some amazing investigative journalism here!"

Now was not the time to be mentioning my investigative skills. I had the funny feeling Chuck wouldn't appreciate them.

I said, "Would you just quit it?" and bent down to pick the stuff up.

Andy went, "Whoa. Careful, C-C. Let me do that for you. No sudden movements. I don't want you fainting again."

She got down, scooped up the papers and stuffed them into the folder.

She said, "We better get going, Chuck. Cyril needs to get a decent night's sleep. I don't want him getting any worse." She handed him the file and put her arm around me. I didn't fight it. I'm pretty sure she was the only thing holding me up.

Chuck went, "Good idea, Andy. I'd look after that boy if I were you. He could get himthelf in real trouble if he'th not careful."

chapter 24

Impostor
A person who engages in deception
under an assumed name or identity.

I was lying in bed. I couldn't sleep. My mind would not shut up. It kept asking the same questions over and over again. Was Chuck Duncan Charles? If he really was some big fancy scientist, why was he working as a janitor? And why hadn't he told anyone he knew Ernest Sanderson?

Did Chuck even *know* he knew him? Maybe he'd lost his teeth in some terrible car accident that left him brain-damaged. Maybe he had amnesia and he didn't even know who he was himself. I mean, it could have happened.

Or I could have just been watching too many bad movies lately.

Had Chuck seen the picture when it fell on the ground? Would it make any difference if he had?

Why was he talking to Biff? Why should I care? Maybe Chuck was telling him to get lost, to quit stalking us. Maybe he was trying to *help* us.

No, that much I knew. Chuck was not a helpful kind of guy.

I still had that stupid project to finish. That's what I should care about. I needed to get some rest. I needed to forget about this stuff.

I tried to force myself into a sleepy state of mind. I tried to replay that scene in my head where Shannondoah kissed me. I tried to think about Mary Mulderry-MacIsaac. I tried to imagine myself skateboarding at one of those professional parks they have down in the States, with Mary and Shannondoah both cheering me on from the sidelines.

All I could think about was Chuck.

Fine.

I turned on the light. I got out the file. Maybe if I spent, like, ten minutes answering some of the questions, I could just forget about it and go to sleep. Maybe there was something in that page I'd printed off the Internet that would straighten the whole mess out for me.

I opened the folder.

I looked at the papers. Everything was neatly handwritten. *Strategies: Malicious Prosecution Suit.*

I must have been really, really tired because it didn't freak me out or anything. I just thought, "Hmm. What's this?" I didn't get it. I flipped through some more papers, thinking, "I wonder where that photo I had went." Then all of a sudden I felt my blood go funny. It was like I had really cold fizzy pop running through my veins. I could feel it working its way to my brain. I was getting goose bumps from the inside out.

I remembered Andy bending down and picking up the papers I'd dropped. I saw her hand the folder to Chuck.

The wrong folder. My folder. The one with his e-mails in it. The one with "his" picture in it.

I was dead.

I grabbed the other folder, threw a jacket over my pajamas and jumped out my bedroom window.

chapter 25

Ab intestato (Latin)
A person who dies without a legal will.

I landed on the fire escape with this giant clang. I froze. Andy's light didn't come on. She must have figured it was somebody else's kid making his break for freedom.

I jumped the rest of the way down and landed on the pavement in a crouch position with my arms out. For a second there, I almost felt sort of cool. It was such an action hero kind of thing to do. I was half hoping somebody had seen me—until I looked down and noticed the leg of my jammies tucked into my sneaker. It kind of brought me back to reality.

I'm not James Bond or Vin Diesel or even Super Worm the Invincible Invertebrate (though that's probably closer). I'm Cyril F. MacIntyre, and I was in a whole, big, giant mess of trouble.

Given the state of my armpits, I presume I ran the whole way to Chuck's place, but I don't remember. It was like my body just slammed right into autopilot. It had to look after itself. All my brainpower needed to go into figuring out what to say to Chuck when I got there. How was I going to explain showing up at his place at eleven o'clock at night? What if he'd already looked in the folder? What was I going to say then?

"It's not my file. It's my lab partner's file. I picked it up by mistake."

Or "Oh? You think that picture with the blacked-out teeth looks like you? Why, I never noticed!"

Or—this was my current favorite—"Why don't you just kill me now and put me out of my misery?"

The security door to Chuck's building was still propped open. That either made me really lucky or really unlucky, depending on how you looked at it. I decided not to look at it at all. I just slipped downstairs and knocked on Chuck's door. I was hoping that inspiration would hit me before Chuck did.

I waited. No answer.

I made myself knock again. I couldn't weasel out of this one. I had to get that file back. I went, "Chuck!" in this kind of loud whisper.

Still no answer.

I knocked harder. I whispered louder. "Chuck! It's me! Cyril!" I banged on the door a few more times.

I got an answer this time. The door to the next apartment flew open and this wrinkly old lady in a pink nightie started shaking a curling iron at me and going, "Hush up with your racket! Why aren't you in bed? I've got half a mind to call the police. Can't you tell the man's not in? What's the matter with you, boy? Decent people are trying to sleep."

I went, "Sorry, sorry" and backed out down the hall. I didn't want any trouble. She was small, but she was armed.

I went outside, and for a second this happy little feeling just sort of wrapped itself around me. I thought, Oh, well. I did my best! I went to his apartment. I knocked. I called. He wasn't there. Nothing I can do about it now.

I started walking home. My mind was trying really hard to do this "Tra-la, tra-la" thing, but my body was still shaking.

Chicken.

Fine. So what? I'm a chicken. I didn't care. At least I was a living, breathing chicken, not the deep-fried nugget I'd be once Chuck—or, for that matter, Andy—found out what I'd been up to.

I walked past the driveway and realized that the windows at ground level belonged to the basement apartments. It wouldn't be hard to figure out which one was Chuck's.

Yeah, so? And then what?

I didn't know.

No point in stopping.

But I was right there. I mean, I may as well at least *look*.

On the other hand, I may as well just keep going.

I kept going.

I stopped. I sighed. I let my head bounce off my chest a couple of times. Then I turned around and walked back to the building.

This was stupid.

Just do it.

I figured Chuck's apartment must be the second one in from the street. I got down on my knees and looked in the window. The lights weren't on and the curtains were pulled shut, but they were a little too narrow. There was a gap between them about as wide as a piece of licorice.

Anyone else would have said, "Okay, fine, I guess I'm not going to be able to see anything. Time to go home and write out my last will and testament," but I didn't.

I stuck my nose right up close to the glass and sort of maneuvered my head around so it didn't get in the way of the streetlight.

I saw something on a table, or at least the corner of something. I was pretty sure it was the file. I had to get a better look.

It was so dark. Was it the file or just an old box?

I hunched on my heels and pushed my face up hard against the window. That turned out to be a mistake.

The window popped open, and I fell headfirst into the apartment.

chapter 26

Break and Enter
A burglary; to break into and enter another's
premises with the intent to commit a crime.

I did a midair somersault and splatted onto the floor with
this giant *Oof*!

The old lady next door banged on the wall and started
screaming about decent people sleeping again. I lay on the
crunchy gray carpet like some stunned snow angel and stared
at the ceiling until the room stopped spinning.

It would have been so easy at that point to just throw in
the towel, draw a chalk outline around myself and wait until
the homicide detectives arrived to pick up the victim, but I
made myself get up anyway.

The lump on the back of my head was about the size of
Chuck's nose, but not, I hope, quite as hairy. I realized I was
going to have to cut a hole in my helmet if I wanted to go
skateboarding any time soon.

Skateboarding. Ha! If Chuck caught me here, I'd be lucky
if I ever walked again.

Oh, right. That reminded me. Smarten up. Get out of
here.

I jumped on the couch and pushed the window closed.
No way was I going to be able to climb out that way. It was

too high up. This wasn't a basement apartment. It was more like a dungeon apartment. I'd have to leave by the door.

What I thought was a file on the table turned out to be just another pizza box. I sort of shuffled things around for a while, but it was clear I wasn't going to be able to find the file in the dark. I turned on a light.

It looked like Chuck picked up his furniture at the same place we did—i.e., the curb on garbage day. He had a couch that sagged in the middle, a three-legged footstool that he used as a coffee table, a busted La-Z-Boy held together with a big zigzag of duct tape, and a card table with an almost matching chair.

Pretty run-of-the-mill stuff for our neighborhood, but Chuck had a much more interesting art collection than the rest of us. He still had the photo of Ernest Sanderson tacked up on the wall. He also had a picture of that Reith guy from the lab, and an 8 × 10 glossy of Shannondoah in her bikini and Miss Gingivitis USA sash.

I got that bugs-crawling-up-your-back feeling.

I didn't like Chuck having Shannondoah's picture on the wall. Lots of guys probably had one, but I knew better than to think Chuck was just another fan. Why was he so interested in her? Revenge?

I was almost afraid to turn around and see what else I'd find. A picture of me? A dead body? Chuck with a big toothless grin—and a bigger gun?

I swallowed. I closed my eyes. I turned around. I made myself open them.

And there it was, smack-dab in front of me. The file was on the card table.

Right next to a brand-new laptop.

Did that ever piss me off! My mother was doing Chuck's work for free, the power company was threatening to turn off our electricity, I still hadn't got my stupid long board and he's got a brand-new laptop? Something was wrong with this picture.

I should have just switched the files and beat it out of there, but suddenly this wasn't about survival anymore.

I was mad now. I'd had enough of Chuck. The guy was a fraud, an impostor! I wanted to take him down.

What did "a poor uneducated boy from backwoods Nova Scotia" need a laptop for? I turned it on to find out.

While I was waiting for it to boot up, I scoped the apartment. My first thought was Chuck must *live* on Railroader's Pizza. (Another thing I hated him for.) I love them—especially their Hawaiian-Greek combo with the double cheese crust—but even I couldn't have hoovered back that many. There were boxes everywhere.

The thing that got me, though, was that most of the boxes looked brand-new. Clean. No grease stains. No rubberized cheese strings. It's like they were straight from the factory.

What was Chuck—a collector or something? Did he think pizza boxes were going to be worth a load of money some day? Why would anyone stockpile unused pizza boxes?

The computer screen lit up. More reasons to be pissed off. Chuck had all the bells and whistles on the dashboard: Photoshop, LimeWire, a video editing program, you name it. I noticed that there was a CD in the laptop too. I clicked on it.

Surprise. Surprise.

It was my video project.

Well, well, well. Chuck was right after all. There had been a robbery. I'd no doubt find *The Catcher in the Rye* in the apartment and, if he wasn't wearing them himself, Andy's toe rings too.

I was getting madder and madder by the second. Nothing burns me more than having to do my homework twice. This guy owed me big-time. I was going to make him pay.

I opened some of the files on his desktop. News stories about Dr. Ernest Sanderson's visit to Halifax. Some stuff Chuck obviously downloaded off the Internet about industrial cleaning and the history of rural Nova Scotia. Articles on the trial.

Nothing too scary there.

I went on Safari and clicked *History*. (The guy even had high-speed service. Arrgh. Kill. Kill.) I wanted to see what type of sites he'd been looking at.

www.patentlyfalse.org. Okay. That answered one question. I clearly had the right Duncan Charles.

Where else had he been surfing?

www.puttingthedieindiet.com.

www.thiswonthurtabit.com.

www.toxintalk.com

Cute URLs, but that wasn't all they had in common. Seems like Chuck had a keen interest in poison. Made me feel squeamish just thinking about it.

I clicked off. All that big talk about taking Chuck down? I suddenly forgot it. I just wanted to get out of there. I was clearly in way over my head. The guy could keep the computer. Just don't kill me.

The laptop was taking forever to shut down. I tapped my fingers on the card table and looked around. There were notes and papers all over the place, but one, pinned to the wall, kind of jumped out at me.

Douglas "Biff" Fougere it said in Chuck's handwriting. Underneath was Biff's phone number, his home address and—it took me a couple of seconds to figure this out—his work schedule.

Any other time, finding something like that would have completely freaked me out, but not this time.

I had other things on my mind now.

For one, the sound of a key in the door.

chapter 27

All Points Bulletin (APB)
A broadcast issued from one law enforcement
agency to another. It typically contains information
about dangerous or missing persons.

There's always that scene in action movies where an out-of-control helicopter piloted by evil international drug dealers crashes into a Winnebago full of TNT. The hero's usually about two feet away when the whole thing blows up, but it doesn't faze him. He's cool. He just

1. turns his head,
2. assesses how fast the fireball is coming at him,
3. takes five powerful steps, then
4. dives to safety on the underside of a passing car.

Piece of cake.

That's more or less what happened here. Only difference was that after I heard the key in the lock, I

1. turned my head,
2. assessed that I was toast,
3. jumped up and down like a little kid who really needs to pee, then
4. somehow managed to hurl myself into the bedroom without knocking over any furniture or leaving a little telltale puddle on the floor.

The door opened—like, seriously—one nanosecond later.

Chuck was in a good mood. I could hear him whistling. Maybe that's why he didn't seem to notice that I'd left the light on. I flattened myself behind the door, and I just prayed he wouldn't come into the bedroom. (This whole experience suddenly made me feel very religious.)

He came into the bedroom. I was shaking so bad it was making the doorknob rattle. Chuck must be used to things rattling when he stomps into a room. He didn't seem to notice that either.

I heard a slurp, a click-click-smack and an "ahhhh." When Chuck started whistling again, he sounded different. Unless I was mistaken, he sounded like a man with his teeth in. He headed back into the other room.

What was I going to do? I couldn't stay behind the door. He'd find me for sure. I needed a better hiding spot.

I heard the sound of the fridge door sucking open. My guess was Chuck would be looking inside. He wouldn't be looking this way. I made my break for it.

I dove under the bed. It wasn't as good as a passing car, but it was good enough. I was pretty sure he wouldn't spot me here. Chuck couldn't see anything below his belly. He probably hadn't seen his feet in years.

I lay on my back and tried not to gag. I was terrified, but that wasn't the only thing making me queasy. The place was like an underwear burial ground. I guess Chuck must have figured, "Why wash them when you can just kick them under your bed and let them air out for a few days?"

I flicked a couple of pairs aside so I could see what was going on. I made a mental note to disinfect my hands when or if I got out of there.

I turned on my side. Even with the gonch out of the way, I didn't have the best view. Every so often, Chuck's feet would go in and out of the frame when he got up for another snack or something, but I couldn't really see too much above his kneecaps.

Chuck sat down out of sight. (I knew he sat down because I could hear the springs of the La-Z-Boy squeak. To tell you the truth, I almost felt sorry for them. It sounded like someone was stepping on a cat's tail.) Chuck didn't get up for a while. He seemed to be settling in. I rolled over flat on my back and tried to relax.

I'd just about managed to get my heart rate below a thousand beats a minute when the phone rang.

So much for relaxing. I almost went through the roof, by which of course I mean the mattress. The phone was so loud it sounded like it was right beside me.

Apparently it was. It rang again, and I realized it was on the bedside table.

My teeth started shivering even worse than before. It was Andy on the phone. I just knew it. It had to be Andy. She'd looked in my room, seen I wasn't there, and now she was putting out the all points bulletin for me. Chuck would say, "No, no. He's not here," but then he'd think, "Hey...Something's up." He'd look around. He'd realize that the light was left on. He'd notice that the laptop wasn't in exactly the place he'd left it. He'd start sniffing the air and doing that "Fee-fi-fo-fum" thing that homicidal giants and friends of my mother do when they smell an intruder.

I was dead.

The phone rang again.

I could hear the La-Z-Boy scream out in agony when Chuck heaved himself up. He went, "All right. All right. I'm coming."

He answered the phone. "Yeah. What?"

Lovely manners. It's like that old proverb, I guess. You can give a man teeth but you can't make him talk nice.

He stood there scratching and going, "Uh-huh... uh-huh...Large or medium? Okay. I'll be ready. Don't be late. People complain if it's cold. And I don't want complaints. Understood? And another thing. Hear from her yet? Did you leave that flyer at her place like I told you to?...Okay, okay. I'll have to figure out another way to get to her. Maybe we should offer a low-fat special...Yeah? What now?...I told you! I got your money! It'll be here!"

He swore and slammed the phone down.

I didn't know what was going on. Was Chuck running a pizza parlor out of here or something? Sounded like he was taking an order. That would explain the boxes, at least.

This was getting weirder and weirder. On top of every-thing else, was Chuck the genius behind Railroader's choo-choo-chewy crust? Was there nothing this man couldn't do?

He left the room. I started breathing again. I figured he wouldn't be back for a while. If Chuck was making pizza, he was going to have to get cracking. Other than the boxes, it didn't look to me like he had anything ready.

I expected him to head into the kitchen, but he didn't. He went back into the living room and sat down out of sight again.

A good ten minutes must have passed. I heard a couple of squeaks and a few bodily noises (if you know what I mean), but that's all. He might have been cutting the cheese, but it wasn't mozzarella.

There was a knock.

Chuck got up, opened the door, and I knew right away it was a Railroader's Pizza delivery. I recognized the smell. (I consider myself a bit of an expert. I was pretty sure I even knew what kind of pizza it was: all-dressed with anchovies. I'd smelled it plenty of times before. It was Biff's favorite. It was the one he always got when he didn't feel like cooking. Personally, I hated it. I could never manage to pick all the anchovies off. There were always a couple I missed, lurking under the pepperoni, just waiting for the right moment to ambush my poor unsuspecting taste buds.)

Chuck mumbled something to the guy at the door, then walked back into the living room. I figured he was getting his wallet or something. I was sort of surprised when he bent down and opened one of the clean pizza boxes he had stacked all over the place.

I was even more surprised to see that he'd put on big yellow oven mitts to do it. What did he need oven mitts for? The boxes couldn't have been hot. Neither could the pizza. I couldn't remember the last time we ordered take-out pizza and it was still warm by the time it got to our place.

Chuck's back was to me, so I couldn't see exactly what he was up to. I heard the *shush* of delicious crispy dough against fresh cardboard. It seemed weird, but I was pretty sure he'd just slid the pizza into the new box. He dropped the old box on the floor. It popped open, empty.

Chuck went back to the door and started ragging away at the delivery guy. "No! Not like that! Watch it! Watch where you put your hands! Careful with the box!" The guy must have wanted to pound Chuck. I mean, it was just a pizza! Chuck was acting like Picasso himself had whipped it up or something.

Chuck gave the guy one last dig, then slammed the door and clicked all the locks shut.

What was going on? Why did he give the pizza back to the guy? Why did he put it in a clean box? Chuck sure wasn't what you'd call, like, fastidious or anything.

No kidding.

He walked into the room and stopped right beside the bed. Believe me, those were not the toenails of a fastidious person. I've seen groundhogs with cleaner toenails.

I heard him stretch. He yawned. He fiddled around with something for a second. Then his shirt landed on the floor. There was a grunt and a *zzzzzip*, he gave a little wiggle and his pants slid down his legs. He stepped out of them.

I knew what was coming next. I braced myself.

He dropped his underwear and, as I predicted, flicked them under the bed with his toe. They skidded to a stop, still warm and steaming, just in front of my face. If I'd stuck out my tongue—which, believe me, I wouldn't do—I could have touched them. All I could think of was the bubonic plague.

Chuck hopped into bed like some seven-year-old all excited about his new Superman sheets. The mattress gave way and I was pinned to the floor. It's amazing he didn't hear my skull crunch.

My worst nightmare had come true.

From what I could gather, Chuck slept in the nude.

chapter 28

Prosecutor

In criminal law, the government lawyer who charges and tries a case against a person accused of a crime.

The good thing about being stapled under a bed by a huge man is that it gives you time to think. I mean, there wasn't much else I could do. I couldn't fidget. I couldn't chew on my hangnails. I couldn't even breathe too deeply. (My lungs worked okay. I was just terrified of inhaling the guy's boxers.)

Suddenly stuff was becoming really clear to me, not least the value of good personal hygiene.

Chuck Dunkirk was definitely Duncan Charles. He knew Ernest Sanderson.

He was a scientist, so he also knew what would happen if you put an explosive substance on a fire.

In other words, it wasn't an accident. This wasn't some Good Samaritan making some bad decision on the spur of the moment. Chuck killed Ernest on purpose.

Why? That's what I couldn't figure out.

Chuck rolled over and I could feel my bones crumbling like a handful of cornflakes. I wished I'd drunk more milk when I had the chance.

I thought of that university video taken in the lab.

Fame, maybe? Is that what he wanted? It clearly bugged Duncan-slash-Chuck that Ernest was getting all the glory. And that was even *before* the whole Gleamoccino thing hit. I mean, can you believe it? The guy was all put out because he wasn't getting equal airtime on some bad promotional video that nobody was even going to watch.

How sad is that?

Was it plain old jealousy that drove Chuck nuts? Is that what happened to him?

Yikes.

Scary.

I promised myself I would never envy anyone ever again for having a nice skateboard or nice clothes or a normal mother. I didn't want what happened to Chuck to happen to me. I pictured myself twenty years from now, all hairy and toothless and, you know, bloated by jealousy, walking up to Kendall and going hi and him going, like, "Who are you?" I mean, that's what it must have been like for people who hadn't seen Chuck in twenty years. He and Duncan didn't even *look* like the same guy anymore.

It suddenly hit me.

I would have conked myself in the head if I could have moved my hand.

Like, duh. Of course! If you planned to kill someone, would you want to be recognized? Chuck didn't *want* to look like Duncan! That's why he left his teeth out. That's why he grubbed himself up, let his hair and beard go, packed on the weight. That's why he stole my video. He must have thought I was onto him.

Everything was falling into place.

And that's why he did that whole publicity-shy thing too. He wasn't humble—no news there—he was just being careful. He wanted to make extra sure no old lab buddy heard about Ernest Sanderson's death on *Inside Edition* and saw past Chuck's disguise.

He pulled up his hood, covered his face, laid low. It made him look good when he was still a hero—not wanting to take all the credit and everything—and it didn't look that strange once he became a suspect either. Everybody hides their face on the way into court. Nobody wants their busdriver or their barista or their second cousin seeing them on TV and thinking they're a criminal.

Chuck was lucky, too, that cameras aren't usually allowed in Canadian courts. All anybody ever saw of him from the trial were those sketches they put on the news. No one would recognize him from one of those. No one would recognize their own *mother* from one of those.

But Shannondoah…That's different. She was in the court. Chuck couldn't hide his face there. Had she recognized him? Is that why she was doing all that research? Because she'd figured something out about him?

Maybe.

Chuck started snoring away like Frankenstein with a sinus problem. I was just waiting for the old lady next door to start pounding on the wall again. (If that racket didn't wake her up, nothing would.)

No, on second thought, I was pretty sure Shannondoah hadn't recognized Chuck—for two reasons. One: The age gap. Shannondoah was probably still in diapers when Chuck and Ernie worked together.

And two: The whole trial would have been different if she had recognized him. I'm almost positive Shannondoah would have told the prosecution lawyer that Chuck wasn't the do-gooding stranger he claimed to be. The lawyer would have no doubt brought that up in court. He would have sniffed around until he found out something that had happened between Chuck and Ernie—an argument, an IOU, a missing sea louse, anything—and then the lawyer would have tried to convince the jury that that was Chuck's motive for killing Ernest.

And if Chuck had a motive for killing Ernest, if he *meant* to kill Ernest, he probably wouldn't have been charged with manslaughter. He would have been charged with murder.

Okay. So what *did* Shannondoah know then?

She knew something. Or, at least, she suspected something. What?

That note of hers I'd found. What had she written on it?

Frankly, when I'd seen it, I'd studied it more for her perfume than for her research. I tried to picture the paper, read it in my mind. There was something about flammability and fire extinguishers and e-mail and…what else?

Think. What else did I remember?

Blond hair. Green eyes. Big laugh.

That's helpful.

Traffic court. She'd written *traffic court*, I was pretty sure of it. Why?

What was it about traffic court?

Biff!

Did Biff run into Ernest at court? Is that what happened? Ernest had all those tickets from speeding down Spring Garden Road. Had Biff been on duty when Ernest appeared in front of the judge?

Maybe that was the connection between Biff and Chuck!

Did Biff tell Chuck that Ernest was there? Did Biff, like, stake Ernest out for Chuck? Make it easy for him?

Was that why he was staking out our place?

I remembered that dinner we had, that look that went between Biff and Chuck. It was funny at the time. Now it wasn't funny at all.

Those guys had been in this together right from the beginning! Just the thought of it made my blood start to, like, throb. It was as if my head had turned into this giant pulsating blob or something.

It was so cruel. It was so mean. Biff had never loved Andy! He might never even have liked her. He'd just been using her. He must have seen her in court or something. He must have heard what a nut she was when it came to that do-gooder stuff. He must have known that all you had to be was some kind of poor oppressed person—some, say, uneducated janitor, for instance—and she'd take your case on, no questions asked.

I thought back to the first time we saw that article in the paper about Chuck. How had we noticed it? Had Biff brought the newspaper to the table? Had he kind of pushed it toward Andy? Was it a setup?

And why did they want Andy on the case so bad anyway?

Was there something about the case that would have scared off a, like, *reasonable* lawyer?

I didn't know. I couldn't remember. I couldn't think. I was so mad. I wanted to kill them.

I wanted to kill Biff most of all. He hurt Andy. He broke her heart. He did it on purpose! I didn't care how big he was. I didn't care that he was "an officer of the court." That was my mother he messed around with. I started to think Andy was right after all. He was a bad, bad guy.

Chuck suddenly lurched up in bed, grinding me into the floor. He turned on the light. He groaned. He scratched. He leaned down hard on my head, then pushed himself up off the bed. (I was going to have a face like an angelfish by the time he was done with me.) He wandered down the hall, went into a room and closed the door. I heard water—at least I think it was water—running.

He was in the bathroom! This was my chance. I slithered out from under the bed and power-crept to the front door. I had my hand on the knob when I remembered the file. I could hear Chuck humming. I hoped he was in there for the long haul. I deked back to the card table and switched the folders.

I was halfway down the street before my heart caught up with me.

chapter 23

Stalking

Any repetitive approach behavior done by one party
that makes another fear for his or her safety.

A ndy was sleeping like a baby when I got back. She hadn't even noticed I was gone.

Biff, though, was another story. I peered out the front window. He was there again. I saw him move in the shadows.

That's all I needed.

I picked up the phone and dialed 9-1-1.

"We have a stalker," I said.

I waited until the police came to arrest him. Biff seemed to argue with them for a while. Then they cuffed his hands behind his back. Just before they pushed him into the squad car, he looked up at the window.

I gave him a big thumbs-up.

One down, and one to go.

chapter 30

Patent
A legal document issued by a government to an inventor. As the owner of the patent, the inventor has the right to keep any other person from making, using or selling the invention covered by the patent anywhere in the country.

The next morning I told Andy I was too sick to go to school. Usually I have to prove I just punctured a lung or lost a limb to get away with that, but this time she fell for it. I must have looked terrible. Near-death experiences can do that to you, I guess.

As soon as Andy left, I got to work. I found Shannondoah's note in my jeans, ransacked the apartment until I scrounged enough money for lunch—as usual these days, there wasn't a thing to eat in the kitchen—then raced down to the library.

Shannondoah said she was there every day. I hoped she meant it. We needed to talk.

Gamers. Homeless guys. The Old Tars Senior Citizens' Book Club. All the usual suspects were there, but no Shannondoah.

I asked the librarian if he'd seen her. He squinted at me like I was moving in on his territory but finally talked. "She was just here a second ago. Said she had an appointment on Spring Garden Road. You could probably cat—"

By the time he said "—cher," I was out the door.

Left to the courthouse, right for everything else.

I chose right. I saw the sun sort of *ping* off that blond hair of hers. She was a good block ahead but not covering much ground in those high heels. I started deking and dodging my way toward her through the pack of people heading downtown.

I got caught on the wrong side of the lights at Queen Street and she gained some ground on me. I really had to boot it when the *Walk* sign came on.

I hollered, "Shannondoah!" She kept going. I didn't know if she heard me.

I hollered, "Shannondoah!" again, this time at the top of my lungs. She heard me. (Trust me. She heard me. People in Tibet heard me.) She turned around. She tilted her head and flashed one of those floodlight smiles of hers. She stopped and waited for me to catch up.

She gave me this naughty-boy look. She went, "Now, how did you know my name?"

I went, "Ah…"

Right. Oh yeah. I forgot about that. We'd never introduced ourselves. As far as I was supposed to be concerned, she was just some lady I ran into at the library.

Looking back, I realize I should have just said, "I recognize you from the paper" or something like that—but I didn't.

I got myself all worried that she'd be suspicious if she found out I knew stuff about her. She'd put two and two together and realize I was Andy's son. She wouldn't talk to me anymore. She wouldn't believe I was on her side.

I panicked. I was standing there with my mouth open, trying to think of other reasons a kid like me would know her name. I could only come up with one.

The worst possible one.

Next thing I knew, I was raising an eyebrow at her like I was some underaged lounge lizard and going, "I made it my business to know your name. You're a very attractive woman."

Normally, I guess, you wouldn't want someone to laugh when you said a thing like that, but I was so relieved that she did. There was at least a chance she thought I was joking.

She went, "Why, aren't you sweet! Now what are you doing downtown on a school day?"

Perfect entrée. "Ah…you left this at the library." I handed her the note. "Thought it might be…*important*." I pictured her opening it up and kindly explaining what each item on the list meant, one by one.

"Oh, thank you!" she said. "I was wondering where that got to."

She put it in her purse and kept walking.

So much for the entrée. How was I going to bring it up now?

She kept chitchatting about the weather. It took me about a block and a half to mentally get as far as "There's something I want to, you know…like, ask you…" when she suddenly stopped and said, "Well, it's been nice talking to you. This is where I'm going."

No, she couldn't go yet. I had to find out what she knew about Chuck.

Do something, Cyril.

Do it now.

Now!

I went, "Oh yeah? Really? Funny. Me too." I looked up and realized we were standing outside the Sensual You Beauty Spa.

She gave my shoulder a little slap and said, "Well, I'll be! Aren't you the new man? I couldn't get my husband to try any of this girly stuff!"

Girly stuff. Okay. Not ideal but, whatever. I couldn't let that stop me. I did a quick check around to make sure no one from school was looking, and then I headed in behind her.

It was one of those groovy-cool places where everything is white and shiny, and all the people who work there look like they should have their own TV show. Shannondoah fit right in.

I didn't.

The receptionist went, "Hey, Shannondoah! You're a little early today. Make yourself comfortable, and I'll tell Lawrence you're here. In the meantime, can I get you a cucumber infusion or a yam smoothie or anything good like that?"

Shannondoah sighed in that nice way of hers and said, "I'm fine, I'm fine." She sat down in the waiting room.

The receptionist turned to me and said, "And what can I do for you, sir?" I hadn't thought that far yet. All I really wanted was a few more minutes with Shannondoah.

I was going to say "A haircut," but I checked the price list sitting on the counter. A haircut cost sixty bucks! That was ridiculous. I didn't have sixty bucks worth of hair on my entire body.

Now what?

It would be way too embarrassing to say "Nothing, thanks," especially with Shannondoah sitting right there.

I stood there, stunned and sweaty, like the kid at the head of the cafeteria lineup who agonizes between the chicken wrap and the hot hamburger special as if he's trying to figure out which one to ask to the prom.

The receptionist scratched her neck with a pencil and tried not to look irritated.

I scanned the price list again. There was only one thing there for under ten bucks. That's about what I had in change. I didn't care what it was. I pointed to it. "I'll have, you know, that," I said.

She smiled and lifted her eyebrows way up. She leaned in close to me. She whispered, "Sure. No problem. Lawrence can do you too if you don't mind waiting."

I took a seat next to Shannondoah. Time to man-up. No use putting it off any longer.

I said, "So, like, what are you here for?"

She laughed. "You're not supposed to ask things like that in a spa. You could get an answer you'd rather not hear!"

I went, "Oh, no, sorry. I meant, what are you in *Halifax* for?"

She laughed again. "Now how did you know I wasn't from these parts?" She nudged me in the ribs with one of those long nails of hers. "Sounds like you've been doing your research too!"

I went, "Ah, yeah, sort of," and blushed. Luckily, she thought it was cute.

"I guess you know who my husband was then," she said.

I nodded. She smiled but in a kind of sad way.

"I was here for the trial."

I went, "Oh, right… But that was ages ago, wasn't it? How come you're still here?"

She looked deep into my eyes, reached over and took my hand, then said, "Well, you're very attractive too, you know."

My heart thumped. She let out a big laugh. I started laughing too. She totally nailed me.

"Seriously," I said.

"I am serious, honey! You're a very attractive young man. But you're right. That's not why I'm still here. I'm still here frankly because…well…I don't know…something just doesn't smell right."

I went, "You're not still talking about me, are you?"

That made her laugh too. Good. Couldn't hurt.

She went, "No, no, you're fine, darlin'. I meant something's fishy, you know."

"Like what?" I said.

She moved her lips around like "Should I tell him or shouldn't I?" I opened my eyes wide and tried to look all innocent and harmless.

I could see this smile sort of passing under her face as if she wasn't totally falling for it but, like, whatever.

She didn't say anything for quite a while. Then she went, "Do you know anything about the trial?"

"Not a lot," I lied. "Someone supposedly tried to save your husband from a fire or something, but he died and they charged the guy with manslaughter. Something like that."

She put her magazine on the coffee table and took a big breath. "Yeah, that's more or less it. Chuck Dunkirk? The guy charged with killing Ernest? He got off, you know. I guess the jury figured he panicked and threw the stuff on the fire without realizing it would explode."

"How do you feel about that?" I said.

She surprised me. "Well, I was sure upset about it at first, but I've sort of come round, I guess. I think the jury did their best with the information they had. I mean, it's true. He could have just panicked. I don't know what I'd do if I saw a fire. Maybe I'd go and do the same thing…"

This wasn't going where I hoped it was going to go.

"So what's fishy then?" I said.

Shannondoah pushed back her hair and looked up at the ceiling for a second. "Well, it's just that the more I thought about it, the more I wondered why there was even a fire in the first place. Sea lice—that's what my husband was working on—they aren't flammable. Believe me, if they were I would have set fire to them ages ago! I hated those ugly little things. I don't know what Ernie saw in them. All I know is that he wouldn't be doing anything with a fire around them. There'd be no reason."

Sounds like Chuck hadn't figured this out as well as he thought he had.

"And another thing," she said. "Why wasn't there a fire extinguisher? Why weren't there lots of them? This was a lab, for goodness sake! Labs always have fire extinguishers. They have to. There are laws about these things, you know..."

She was on a roll now.

"But there's something that bothers me even more than that. The stuff the guy threw on the fire was called Power Powder. He was using it to clean the floors. That's what I don't get. Why did the university still have it? That company had gone out of business ages ago. You want to know why? Because the stuff exploded all the time!"

She put her hand over her mouth and turned away for a second. I should probably have just dropped it there, but I couldn't. She was my best chance for figuring out what was going on here. I convinced myself I was doing it for the both of us.

I waited a second. Then I said, "So, um, what do you think happened? Do you think this Chuck guy was involved somehow? That he did something on purpose?"

She was poking at her eyelashes with her fingernails. Her mascara had gotten wet, but she was acting like this was just a regular touch-up.

"No, I don't think so. At least, not anymore. He's just some poor working guy, trying to make a living. Why would he do that?"

My heart kind of sank. She'd fallen for Chuck's big act too.

She kept going. "I have two theories. Chuck Dunkirk honestly tried his best to save Ernie. He couldn't find a fire extinguisher and didn't know any better than to throw that stuff on the fire. If that's the case, then I think we should be suing the university. I've looked into it. I found a couple of legal sites on the Internet—thanks to you." She reached over and patted my hand. I tried to concentrate on what she was saying anyway. "Unless I misunderstood something, it's the university's job to make sure their employees are trained and their buildings are safe. There shouldn't even have been any Power Powder around."

That didn't help me much. "What's your other theory?" I said.

"That this isn't all it seems to be." She did that "woo-hoo spooky" thing with her hands and laughed. "I know that sounds foolish. My lawyer looked at me like I'm some airhead when I said that to him. Maybe I am. I didn't actually finish high school—and if you need any proof I'm an airhead, there it is. Quitting school to go into a beauty contest! That's about as dumb as you can get…Anyway. That's beside the point."

She looked at me. "You really want to hear my crackpot theory?"

I nodded.

"Well, you're the first, kiddo. Okay, here goes. I think someone wanted to kill Ernie because of Gleamoccino. They planted that Power Powder there or started the fire or something."

"Who?" I said. "Why?"

"Who? I don't know. Why? Well, it's a stretch, I guess—but I think it has to do with patent protection. You know what a patent is?"

I did but I wasn't going to admit it. She didn't need to know how much I knew. "No, not really," I said.

"I'm not a lawyer—ha, ha, no kidding, eh?—but how can I explain this? A patent, I guess, is just sort of proof that you invented something. If you've got the patent for something, it means you're the only person who can make it or sell it or make money from it. If you've got the patent for something good, you can get really rich off it. Like Ernie and his partner Mike did. Unfortunately, when that happens, all other people see is the money. They don't see all the hard work it took to bring Gleamoccino to market. Ernie told me it took them years before they got something that whitened your teeth without making them fall out first."

I pictured Chuck's gummy mouth going, "He could get himthelf in real trouble if he'th not careful." Something was beginning to come together for me.

Shannondoah told the receptionist that she'd like a cucumber infusion after all; then she kept going.

"Anyway, Ernie had been getting crank calls and letters from some guy for years, claiming he was the real inventor of Gleamoccino and that Ernie had just gotten to the patent office first. Ernie didn't like to worry me about that kind of thing, but I know he ran into him again here in Halifax."

"Really," I said. "Where?" I had a pretty good idea what she was going to say.

"Ernie got in a little trouble for speeding…" She did that sort of "oops" thing with her face and laughed. "He was a bit of a health nut, you know. He wouldn't touch fast food, but he loved fast cars! Anyway, he had to go to traffic court. He came back really, I don't know, agitated. I thought he was just upset because the judge got so mad at him—but it was something else. I found out later that a man had kind of, you know, accosted him. Said something to him. I think it must have been the guy. The guy who wrote the letters. If he knew when Ernie was going to be in traffic court, he could have known when he'd be alone in the lab too."

Missing teeth. The "Patently False" website. Traffic court. It made perfect sense.

Shannondoah was looking down at her hands and twisting her wedding ring around. "I wish I realized earlier how much trouble Ernie was in. Maybe I could have saved him somehow. It's upsetting me so much I can't sleep. I can barely eat. I'm a mess."

She scrunched her face up to keep from crying.

"You're not a mess, Shannondoah," I said. I meant it too. I wasn't just saying that to make her feel better. She wasn't a mess. She was pretty, and she was nice, and she was smart too. Nobody else had figured out what actually happened. I was willing to bet she had.

"You're so sweet," she said. "Almost as sweet as my Ernie." She was squeezing my hand and sniffing back the tears when Lawrence came in.

"Should I come back?" he said.

Yes.

Shannondoah shook her head. "No, no, that's fine. We were just chatting."

Lawrence went, "Your facial treatment's going to take some time, Shannondoah. Mind if I do your friend first? A hot lip waxing should only take a second, especially with the little bit of peach fuzz he's got."

chapter 31

Cui bono (Latin)

Literally, "To whose benefit?" The phrase is used to suggest that the person or people guilty of committing a crime may be found among those who have something to gain from it.

For the next hour or two, I was more interested in getting a jail sentence for Lawrence than for Chuck. I mean, what sadistic maniac came up with that waxing idea? You pour boiling hot wax on someone's face, tear it—and most of their lip—off, then charge them ten bucks for the pleasure? The guy's an evil genius.

I'd deal with Lawrence later. Right then, I had to figure out what to do about Chuck.

I was sure now that he was behind it. I mean, it all made sense. Chuck had worked with Ernest and that Mike Reith guy. One of them came up with the idea for Gleamoccino. Who knows? It could even have been Chuck. He was the one missing the teeth.

In any event, Ernest and Mike patented the idea. They got rich. Chuck got mad. It took him years, but somehow or another he wangled things so he was alone in a lab with Ernest. He got his hands on some old Power Powder. He knew it would blow up good. He threw it on the fire and made it look like it was all a big accident.

The obvious thing for me to do now would be to call the police.

And admit I'd broken into the guy's place, rifled through his stuff, checked his Internet history?

No, I don't think so. I wanted them to arrest Chuck, not me.

And, anyway, what proof did I have that he did it? Like, real proof? All the pieces fit together, but so what? People make up stories every day that fit together. They still aren't enough to convict a man. I didn't have any fingerprints. I didn't have any blood spatters or eyewitness accounts. All I had was a pretty good hunch.

Generally speaking, judges don't take too kindly to hunches.

And there was another thing that was bugging me too. Even if I had evidence—good, solid evidence—proving that Chuck did it, I wasn't sure it would make any difference. Something I remembered from law school was sort of coming back to me. Some legal principle.

Res Judicata. That was it.

If it meant what I thought it meant, we were too late. No one could convict Chuck of killing Ernest, even if we'd captured it live on CNN.

I couldn't stand it.

I had the sinking feeling that Chuck was going to get off scot-free.

chapter 32

Search Warrant

A court order issued by a judge or magistrate that authorizes law enforcement to search a person or location for evidence of a criminal offense and seize such items.

Kendall didn't like my idea, but he went along with it anyway. That's what I liked about him.

"You're sure Chuck did it?" he said.

I nodded and put a CD in the camera.

"And you're sure this is the only way we can get him?"

No, I wasn't sure. Some brilliant legal genius could maybe have come up with something else, but this was the best I could do. I nodded again.

"Yeah," I said. "I'm sure. There's no way he'd be convicted. I called Atula and asked."

Kendall's eyeballs nearly bugged out of his head. "You told Atula what you're planning on doing?! And she let you?"

I snorted. "No! What? You think I'm crazy! Of course I didn't tell her. I just kind of, you know, *hypothetically* explained the situation as if I had some big school project to do on lying homicidal maniacs. I asked her if, under the circumstances, the principle of *res judicata* would apply. She said yes, hypothetically, that is."

Kendall shrugged and went, "Well, I guess we have no choice then."

We did have a choice, of course. We could have called the police and hoped they'd believe some fifteen-year-old kid. Maybe they'd just pretend not to notice I got most of my so-called evidence when I illegally broke into Chuck's apartment.

We could have just given up. We could have said, "That's the way it goes," and forgotten all about it.

We could have done a lot of other things, I guess, and part of me really, really wanted to, but I just couldn't. I couldn't let Chuck Dunkirk get away with murder. I had to get him while I could.

"Nope," I said. "We've got no choice. So—should we just do it or what?"

Kendall lifted his hand like, yup, go ahead.

I tried not to shake. I tried to act as cool as Kendall. I picked up the phone and called Chuck. I asked him if he minded if I came by and showed him my project again. I needed his advice. I had a few questions I wanted to ask him.

He was most welcoming. I wasn't surprised.

He loved being the know-it-all.

And he no doubt had a few questions for me himself.

chapter 33

Alias

An assumed name.

"Well, well, well," I said. "I see you've redecorated."
The place was spotless. The laptop was gone.
The pizza boxes must have been put out with
the recycling. The pictures of all Chuck's buddies were tucked
away. The place looked like a real janitor might actually have
lived there. Even if I had called the police, they wouldn't have
found anything now.

Chuck smiled. He hadn't redecorated his gums.

"Come in, come in," he said. "Are you hungry? I juth
had thome pete-tha and there are a few thlithes left if you'd
like one."

When had I eaten last? I couldn't remember. I'd had
so much to do that day to get ready. I was starving. I could
tell from the smell it was my favorite, the Hawaiian-Greek
special, but I said, "No, thanks," anyway. I was having enough
trouble swallowing as it was.

"Tho, what have you got for me?" Chuck was doing his
jolly department-store Santa thing. I practically expected him
to ho-ho-ho and put me on his knee.

"Well," I said, "I'm just about finished my project and I wanted to make sure I had the facts right. Would you mind checking it for me?"

Chuck went, "Gee, I'd love to. I don't know how much help I'll be. I'm juth a poor uneducated boy from backwoodth Nova Thcotia, you know."

We both smiled at that. He wasn't even pretending that hard anymore.

I looked around for an outlet. I found one near the window and plugged in the video camera. Perfect.

"Mind if I open the window just a crack?" I said. "I'm a little hot." I even had the sweat stains to prove it.

Chuck smiled and waved his hand like, Go ahead. We sat down on the couch. I put the video camera on the coffee table and twisted the viewfinder so we could both see it. He was a little too close for comfort, but what could I do?

"All ready?" I said.

"Roll 'em," he said.

It was a little different than the version he'd seen before. For starters, the opening line was: "Chuck Dunkirk—AKA Duncan Charles—killed Ernest Sanderson in cold blood."

chapter 34

Attempted Murder

Attempting to kill someone deliberately or recklessly
with extreme disregard for human life.

I t was kind of annoying. I'd worked really hard updating
my project, but Chuck didn't even bother to watch it.
We barely got to the part about him changing his name
and tracking Ernest down to Nova Scotia, when he leapt on
me. (He was much more agile than I thought he was.)

That came as a bit of a surprise. I thought I was going to
have a little more time to set up my trap.

He had his hands around my neck and was bashing my
head against the floor. I tried to fight him off, but what a joke
that was.

It dawned on me that I had forgotten to give Kendall a
cutoff signal. Big mistake.

It was looking hopeless. I heard angel voices. I was
starting to realize that I wasn't going to be able to follow
through with my plan—which, among other things, had
included living to adulthood.

I wasn't going to be Shannondoah's hero. I wasn't going
to break that all-important five-foot-five mark. I was going to
die in some grubby basement apartment at the hands of one
of Andy's creepy clients.

The bump I'd given myself the night before must have looked like an ingrown hair next to the one Chuck was giving me now. That white light was starting to seem really, really tempting.

Oh well, I thought, it's not a total loss. At least we'll be able to get Chuck on a murder charge after all.

Too bad it's going to be for murdering me.

For just a second there, I felt kind of noble. You know, the ultimate sacrifice and everything. I saw the headlines in the paper, imagined Eva Jackson doing the *Breaking News* story, pictured the flag at half-mast at our school.

I was almost enjoying it until I got to the part where my poor broken-hearted mother was weeping at my grave. Then suddenly everything changed.

Did that ever make me mad! Why was I the one dying around here? Andy was the one who dragged me into this lawyer stuff. I didn't like it. I never had. I just wanted to skateboard. Hang out. Goof around. If she hadn't tried to turn me into some little legal scholar, I wouldn't be having my brain bashed in right now.

This was her fault.

All her fault.

As usual.

No way was I going to die at fifteen for a stupid little thing like justice.

I had to fight. I couldn't give up.

I got this burst of strength. It wasn't superhuman strength or anything handy like that, but it was enough. I bent Chuck's thumbs back a millimeter or two. My windpipe popped open. I sucked in this little whistle of air, looked him right in the eye and said what I needed to say.

"*Res judicata.*"

chapter 35

Double Jeopardy

A legal concept referring to the idea that a person charged with a crime and found not guilty cannot be charged with the exact same crime again. In Canada, double jeopardy is often referred to as "one time around."

I had to kind of croak it out three times, but it finally worked. Chuck stopped choking me. I knew he wouldn't be able to stand not knowing what it meant.

"What?" he said.

I rubbed my neck with my hand and swallowed a few times just to make sure everything was still in working order. "Res. Ju-dee-cat-ah," I said. "It means 'the thing has been decided' in Latin."

He growled, "Tho what?" and went to grab me by the neck again.

I got my hand in there first. "In other words," I said, "you got away with it."

He looked me up and down like I was trying to sell him hot watches off the street or something. He didn't believe me.

"Seriously," I said. "It's a very important legal principle. It means you can't try a person twice for the same crime."

He really wanted to keep strangling me, I could tell. (I'd seen that look on Andy's face before.) But I just kept talking and he managed to control himself.

"You've heard of double jeopardy?" I said. I didn't know if he had or not, but he nodded anyway. No way would he admit he didn't know something, especially to a little pest like me. "Same thing. If you get tried in a court of law and you get found not guilty, they can't try you again for the same offense even if there's new evidence. It doesn't matter that you killed Ernest Sanderson. You're a free man, Chuckie!"

He laughed at me like I was a moron. "You're wrong. Verdictth get appealed all the time."

I sat up. "Do you mind getting off me?" I said. "My legs are going to sleep." He moved away but kept close enough that he could still clobber me if he needed to.

"Appealing a verdict is different," I said. I was on kind of shaky ground here. It had been a long time since I sat through a law class. I tried to remember what Atula had told me. "Cases can be appealed if the judge or the lawyer made a mistake in the law. You know, say the judge told the jury something wrong, or one of the lawyers didn't follow the rules, that kind of thing. But nothing like that happened in your case. Nobody made a legal mistake. The jury looked at the evidence and decided you weren't guilty—even though, of course, you are."

I thought he was going to haul off and hit me, but I redeemed myself.

"I mean, you're a genius! You tricked them all. You got to kill Ernest Sanderson *and* you got off without a scratch. You won big-time, Duncan! Oh, sorry. Mind if I call you Duncan? That's your real name, right? Duncan Charles?"

I could see a smile sort of beginning to creep onto his face.

"Yeah. Fine. Call me Duncan. My mother alwayth did."

I patted him on the back. "You deserve to be congratulated. Honest. You really got Ernest good for stealing your Gleamoccino idea…"

Chuck sort of chuckled. "You're right. I did, didn't I?"

Now I was coming to the important part. It was just a hunch, but I had to try anyway. It was either going to work or it wasn't.

"Tell me. There's one more thing I just have to know. Was killing Ernest better for you than killing Mike Reith? I mean, was it more—say—satisfying?"

Chuck thought about it. "You know, I think it wath. Killing Mike wath almotht too eathy for me. He ate a lot. Poithoning him wath a piethe of cake. I jutht thprinkled a little on hith muffin every day for a couple of month and he wath gone. But Ernie wath tho careful with hith food. He uthed to thay, 'Fatht food will kill you!' I thought, if only! It would have made it a lot eathier for me. I could have killed both of them at the thame time."

I tried to give him one of those, "Oh, that's too bad" looks. He shook his head and shrugged.

"Then Ernie got rich, and I couldn't get near him. I tried threatening him, but it didn't do any good. I had to come up with a new idea. In the end, killing him took yearth to pull off. Funnily enough, that jutht made it all the more enjoyable. I felt like I accomplithed thomething. That all the yearth I thpent brooding and planning were worth it…"

"Well, that's great, Chuck. You're no doubt an inspiration to deranged murderers everywhere. So—is your little killing spree over now? Can you finally relax?"

"Yeah," he nodded. "Jutht about."

"You must be looking forward to putting your teeth in again."

He laughed. "No kidding. I'm looking forward to going to the all-you-can-eat rib night at the Flamingo. I hear it'th very good!"

I went, "Oh, yeah. It's great." As if I would know. Like we could afford to go to the Flamingo. I got up to leave. No use staying around chatting. I had what I needed.

He grabbed me by the arm. "Hold on there," he said. His face had gone back to its old creepy Chucky self. "What are you planning to do with that video?"

"Oh, this?" I said. I took it out of the camera. "Here. You can have it. I'm not doing anything with it."

He had the CD in his hand, but he still wasn't happy. "I thought it wath for thchool. What are you going to turn in if I've got it?"

"Don't worry. I'll use something else. I just wanted to show this to you. I'm kind of like you that way. I just like to know that I'm right."

His face sort of loosened up at that. He reached over and patted me on the shoulder. Oh, yeah. We were great buddies.

"Sure you don't want thome pete-tha before you go?" he said.

I shook my head. I was dying to see if Kendall got it all on video.

chapter 36

K endall was still crouched down by the basement
window when I came out. He picked up his camera
and just, like, beamed at me. I can't remember the
last time I saw him so excited.

He went, "You just got an A on your video project, my
friend!"

Having oxygen cut off from my brain for a few minutes
seemed almost worth it. "Excellent," I said. "That's all
I want. An A for me—and twenty-five years to life for
Chuck."

I thought we could get it too. My plan had worked.
We had Chuck confessing to the murder of Mike Reith on
video. We could probably get him a few years more for trying
to kill me too.

I was feeling pretty good. My only problem now would
be breaking this to Andy. She wasn't going to be too happy
with me for pooching her big malicious prosecution suit. I
figured I better start buttering her up now.

We found a pay phone that actually worked a couple of
blocks from the apartment, and I called her. I expected Andy

to be really mad at me for not being home in bed after I told her how sick I was, but she sounded fine.

Not surprisingly, it was because of food.

She went, "Oh, hey, Cyril. You on your way home? Better hurry. You're not going to believe this, but Chuck sent us over a pizza this afternoon. You know, to thank me for all the work I've done for him. It's sooooo good." She loved taunting me. "Railroader special. Mm-Mm-Mm. Your favorite. Yummmm yum…Hear that, Cyril?" She started chomping right in the phone. "That's me digging my teeth into its choo-choo-chewy crust. Nyah-nyah-nyah. I'm going to eat it all. Better hurry if you want…What the *beep*?"

Suddenly she was screaming at someone at the top of her lungs. She dropped the phone. I could hear plates smashing and chairs falling over and her screeching and a man's voice.

I'm used to Andy's mood swings, but this seemed a little extreme even for her.

I dropped the phone and took off.

The whole way home all I could hear was Chuck's voice. *He ate a lot. Poithoning him wath a piethe of cake.*

chapter 37

Extenuating Circumstances
Surrounding factors which make a crime appear less serious or without criminal intent, and thus deserving a more lenient punishment.

Biff had Andy in a headlock, but she wasn't giving in easy. She was kicking him and punching him and screaming, "Give me back my *beeping* pizza!"

I didn't want her to have the pizza—but I didn't want Biff to get her either. Kendall and I both piled on top of him. I could tell by the look on Andy's face she was worried she was going to have to fight all three of us for the pizza.

Next thing I knew there were sirens and police barging in, and the neighbors were all craning their necks to get a good look at what was happening.

The cops picked Kendall and me off the pile like we were lint on a sweater. I figured they were going to arrest Biff—I mean, he was a stalker after all—but they just helped him up and dusted his jacket off.

Andy was standing there, rhyming off the list of charges that should have been brought against Biff: break and enter, theft, assault and battery, libel, disturbing the peace, treason... She was just starting to make them up now.

The big cop—or should I say, the bigger cop—must have known her from court or something. He went, "Excuse me,

Andy, but I think you owe Deputy Sheriff Fougere here an apology. I believe the man just saved your life by taking that pizza from you."

Andy was in no mood for this type of stuff. "Yeah, right. The trans fats were going to kill me or something? Please."

"No," I said, "your client was."

chapter 38

Actus reus (Latin)

Literally, "Guilty act." The actual crime that is committed
rather than the intent leading up to the crime.

*R*es Judicata. It was true what I said to Chuck. You
can't be tried for the same crime twice.

I admit, though, I was wrong about a lot of other
stuff.

Like Biff, for instance. He wasn't stalking us. He was
protecting us. He'd figured this whole thing out long before
I did.

He had met Chuck in traffic court, like I suspected.
He was the deputy sheriff who saw Chuck accost Ernest
Sanderson there.

By the time Biff came over to see what the matter was,
Chuck was walking away from Ernest. All he heard Chuck
say was, "Don't you worry. You'll get your just desserts."
Ernest looked shaken up, but he waved it off. Biff figured it
was no big deal. He sees worse than that every day in court.
He forgot about it.

Then, months later, Chuck came to dinner at our place.
Biff didn't know where he'd seen him before, but there was
something sort of familiar about the guy. He didn't know
what it was.

It wasn't until he brought out the cheesecake that something clicked. Chuck made some joke about "your just desserts." It's not an expression you hear all the time. It all came back to Biff. He remembered the guy in traffic court who'd got all huffy with Ernest. The guy definitely had teeth and a decent suit on too, but that didn't fool Biff. He was suddenly sure the guy was Chuck.

Biff remembered the look on Ernest's face too. How white he was. That sold him. Biff realized Chuck wasn't just some Good Samaritan. He guessed that Chuck might have had a reason to kill Ernest. Biff waited until everyone went home before he told Andy his suspicions.

She didn't take it well. Typical Andy. She decided Biff was just another officer of the court who figured if you're poor, you're guilty. She threw him out.

Biff did some research. The more he looked into Chuck Dunkirk, the less he liked the guy. Biff knew his way around the Internet. None of Chuck's stories about growing up in rural Nova Scotia panned out.

Biff worried about us. He started hanging out around our place just to make sure we were all right. He made sure Chuck saw him. Biff wanted him to know he was being watched. He couldn't let us know though. Andy would have had a bird.

All the time, Biff was living on take-out pizza. At first, that's why he thought he was feeling sick. Too much junk food. Then he noticed he got the same delivery boy every time he called Railroader's. Biff recognized him from his days as a sheriff in juvie court. Biff also noticed the kid was suddenly sporting a fancy new watch and some grills on his teeth.

Biff followed the money.

He figured out which window was Chuck's faster than I did. He watched the delivery boy come, saw Chuck switch the pizza into a new box and send it out.

Biff noticed the oven mitts, same as me. It made him wonder why the delivery boy was always wearing gloves too. (Up to that point, he'd figured it was just another one of those weird teen trends.) Biff didn't know what was up, but he sure thought it was suspicious.

Meanwhile, I was getting suspicious too. Of Biff. That chicken dinner had made me sick. Those missing toe rings sure looked like his work. I called the cops on him.

Best thing I ever did.

Biff shared a cell with a murder suspect. They got to talking. The guy couldn't believe how stunned Biff was. "C'mon! Think like a criminal!" he said. "What's the matter with you? The boxes are poisoned!" It didn't make sense to Biff at first. I mean, why wouldn't Chuck just put the poison right on the pizza? But Dino "The Widow-maker" Chisholm had an answer for that too. "Probably has something to do with aftertaste. When you're offing someone slow-like, you can't have them getting suspicious...Or so I'm told."

Things started falling into place. Biff realized that Chuck would have killed me ages ago, but we were too poor for take-out pizza. That's why he made it look like Biff was killing me instead. He sent the chicken dinner over. He rigged that robbery to seem like Biff was behind it too. He got me off the scent.

Luckily, Biff got out on bail just in time to save Andy. After I'd broken into his apartment the night before, Chuck wasn't messing around with little doses anymore. The pizza he sent over that day would have killed a rhino. Chuck obviously wanted to get rid of me as fast as possible. He didn't mind taking Andy out with me.

I had to let her watch the video Kendall took about ten times before she'd accept that Chuck really was a bad guy. She was pretty bummed out about it for a while, but she recovered. Now she's representing a poor grieving widow— i.e., Shannondoah—in her negligence case against the big bad university.

And as for me? I did get an A on my project.

We celebrated with an extra-large Hawaiian-Greek special. Shannondoah and Biff were the guests of honor.

Vicki Grant is the author of *Quid Pro Quo*, which won the Arthur Ellis Award for Best Juvenile Crime Fiction and was shortlisted for the Edgar Allan Poe Award. She is also the author of *The Puppet Wrangler*, *Pigboy* (Orca Currents), *Dead-End Job* and *I.D.* (Orca Soundings). Vicki lives in Halifax, Nova Scotia.